I0732015

SHAMAN PUNK CRISIS
BOOK I

SHAMAN PUNK PRINCESS

Phoebe An Lee

Library and Archives Canada Cataloguing in Publication

Title: Shaman Punk Princess
Name: Phoebe An Lee, author
Identifiers: ISBN 978-1-7383751-3-4 (ebook) |
ISBN 978-1-7383751-4-1 (paperback) | ISBN 978-1-7383751-7-2 (hardcover)

Shaman Punk Princess

Part I

I

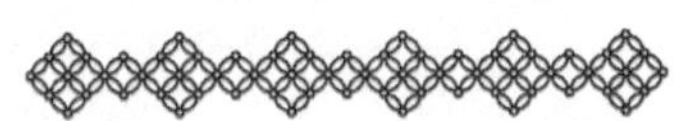

I shouldn't be here.

That was Jinlei's first thought as she roamed the unfamiliar streets. The garish neon signs and strange buildings piercing the sky were all too strange and alien to her. A peculiar animal honked angrily at her. It rolled down its glass eye, and she was surprised to see that it was carrying a person inside when a human head appeared.

"You crazy, lady? Don't you know better than to stand in front of a speeding car?" the man screamed more profanities at her before speeding away.

Car? What's a car? Jinlei was still groggy and disoriented, as if she had just woken up from a bad dream. Her head throbbed. Disjointed images flashed through her mind. The last thing she remembered was her mother's crying face as her mother's hand slipped away from hers in their last parting.

As she wandered the streets with her pounding head, people in bizarre skin-tight black or neon clothing shot her sleazy glances. They seemed to like wearing shiny cow hides in this world. Completely opposite to her beautiful, flowing, blood-spattered silk robes and bejeweled hair ornaments. No wonder they looked at her strangely.

She scared them off with her own menacing glare. She passed by what looked like run-down shops of sorts. In one of the shop windows, a flashing box showing moving pictures caught her eye.

A lovely woman who was more well-dressed than the unwashed people on the streets was making an announcement in the flashing box. Jinlei's eye moved to the bottom of the box. It read, "Today: June 25, 2050. 7:30 PM."

It all made sense now. Her mind flashed back to the day her family came under attack, the chaos and foulness still fresh on her skin. Despite her protests, Jinlei's mother banished her against her will.

It was her dear mother's way of protecting her—by sending her away. Thirteen hundred years into the future.

II

The realization sent Jinlei's head spinning once more. She staggered, barely able to walk a straight line.

"Watch it!" a woman with green hair told her off. The woman was about to shove Jinlei back but changed her mind and walked off, disgusted.

Despite how different she looked, Jinlei knew she could carry herself well and scare off any street riff-raff. Even though she looked like a noble lady, something about her silently commanded to the people to back off. That came from years of training. Even the people back home knew not to underestimate her.

But she knew she shouldn't be roaming the streets in her condition. She needed shelter. Or at least a place to sit and gather her bearings.

Ahead, she saw a few people stream in and out of an unmarked door. She briefly saw the outlines of tables and chairs as the door swung open and shut. It seemed her place of refuge would be a dark and dingy establishment of questionable repute. But beggars couldn't be choosers. She was a beggar now, she supposed. How far she had fallen from the noble house of Ling!

The guard outside the door looked her up and down. She steeled herself. If she had to fight just to have a bit of rest, so be it.

The guard scoffed mockingly. "Go on in, little lady. I guess it's about time they had some entertainment in there." He gave her a knowing wink. She narrowed her eyes at him. She didn't know what exactly he meant, but she made sure he knew she could handle herself. He merely gave her a laugh of derision in return.

Inside, the patrons looked even rougher than the urchins in the streets. Hair in different colors with metal earrings and studs pierced throughout their inked bodies. She took a seat in a corner table, trying to remain invisible. But that was impossible in this crowd.

Mostly, people gave her nasty looks and passed her by. Until one didn't.

The crowd parted as a big brute with snake ink crawling over his arms arrogantly walked around as if he owned the place. He stopped right at Jinlei's table and towered intimidatingly over her.

"That's my seat," he said.

Jinlei shifted uncomfortably.

"Perhaps you can take this seat instead?" she suggested reasonably, pointing to a seat next to her. The establishment wasn't particularly packed and there were a few empty tables and chairs around. The low lights made it somewhat hard to see, but the other patrons deliberately shied their faces away from the oncoming confrontation. Others watched with interest.

"Nah, this is my table, you see," the tattooed man replied in a threatening voice.

Puzzled, Jinlei tried reasoning again with him. "But there was no one here when I came. There are enough seats for both of us. Perhaps we may share the table?"

The big brute slammed his drink on the table. "I don't think you understand. This is *my* table. Everybody knows this is Snakeskin's table. Every night. Until eternity. Capisce?"

"Oh," Jinlei fumbled. "Sorry . . . I-I didn't know . . ."

She got up hastily. But Snakeskin's beefy arm blocked her.

"Nah, you ain't gettin' off that easy, princess. There are rules in this bar. And those rules must be followed."

"Sorry, I didn't know . . ." she said again, this time more alert as she noticed other similarly tattooed men circle around her. "But I shall give you back your table, and I'll be on my way. Thank you very much." She bowed hastily, hoping to scurry out of there without any trouble.

Snakeskin grabbed her arm roughly.

"Like I said. There are rules. You can't get away that easily."

She winced. "Please. What are the rules? I'm sure we can work something out."

"You're right, we sure can." He grinned menacingly. "I'm sure we can find some use for a pretty little thing like you. Don't we, boys?"

The men around her laughed lewdly. Snakeskin, in particular, looked her up and down in a way that made her skin crawl with a million ants. Her first instinct was to gouge his eyes out. But she was still a lady, after all. There will be no gouging. For now.

She willed herself to calm down, took a few deep breaths and said evenly, "Please, let me go. I don't want to cause any trouble."

Snakeskin laughed out loud. "Too late for that, missy. You're coming with us." He pulled her arm forcefully, dragging her along with him.

The fog overshadowing Jinlei's mind suddenly cleared as a sun clears away rainy clouds. She instantly forgot about the fatigue in her bones. She knew exactly what she had to do. But before she could wrestle her arm away, a long link of chains whipped out of nowhere. It wrapped around Snakeskin's arm, pulling his arm free from Jinlei's.

A tall young man with spiked yellow hair dressed in a black

shiny suit wielded his rope of chains as if they were an extension of his own body. "Now, you know that's no way to treat a helpless little lady," he shook his head mockingly at Snakeskin.

Who is he calling helpless? Equally miffed at her so-called 'rescuer' and the stinky inked brute, Jinlei took advantage of the distraction and slammed her fist into Snakeskin's cheek, holding back no punches. Then she twisted Snakeskin's arm and flipped him over, sending him crashing to the ground.

The others came at her all at once. But she saw them all clearly. She spun and maneuvered, expertly fighting as if she knew the intricate dance by heart. She was the master teacher while her students were just learning the dance.

From the corner of her eye, she saw the yellow-haired boy gape at her in surprise as he fought alongside her.

Snakeskin got himself up and growled. "Alright, enough playing. Boys—no more holding back just because she's a woman. Take the boy too."

Snakeskin's gang took out their knives and other weapons—black things that buzzed and gave off blue currents. Jinlei had never seen such a thing before. But no matter. All she had to do was not let the weapons touch her.

She herself was not without her own weapon. She reached into her waist sash and flipped open the two fans tucked into it—beautifully decorated with birds and flowers. The perfect concealed weapon for a noble lady, made with metal spokes and sharp blades at the ends.

As they slashed their knives at her, she slashed back.

"AAAARRGGHHH!!" the men yelled out as the bladed fans made cuts all over their bodies.

She elbowed one guy in the eye, followed with a jab to the ribs and a slash across his legs. He fell down easy, taking another with him.

She smirked. These so-called thugs were amateurs compared to her.

She spun and kicked and slashed her way to what would look like her victory. Until she made a fatal mistake.

A blade came at her. She successfully maneuvered out of the way. But the blade was just a cover. She failed to see the concealed black weapon in the assailant's other hand. He jabbed the weapon at her side. Painful currents shot at her waist and rapidly spread all over her body.

Jinlei let out a painful breath. She was too arrogant and let her guard down.

It was as if she had been struck by lightning. Every muscle in her body seized up, unable to move. She instantly collapsed to the ground. Hot lightning currents ran all over her as if every cell in her body was on fire. Despite her vast martial arts training, she couldn't help a tear escape from her eye.

Is this the end? she thought. She gasped for air, trying to fan the burning sensation in her body. The painful, shooting heat swarmed the very top of her head to the very end of her toe.

Somewhere around her, she heard the sound of clinking chains. The next thing she knew, she was being lifted up. She tried to struggle, but she had no control over her own body. It was the most terrifying sensation she had ever felt. To not be able to fight back.

Where are they taking me? she wondered before everything went black.

III

White spots filled Jinlei's vision at first.

"... I think she's coming to ..." she heard a distant voice say.

She tried moving her fingers first, then her hands. It seemed she had control of her body again. She blinked a few times to clear her vision and shot straight up, ready for a fight, her hands balled into fists.

"Hey, hey, hey! Woah there! Easy, easy ..." an unfamiliar face tried to pacify her. The stranger had purple hair and glasses. Her hands were raised in a sign of peace.

Jinlei calmed down, realizing that the thugs from earlier were gone, and she was ... where *was* she? She was in a small, dark room with patched-up walls and dirty floors. There was nothing else in the room except the soft bed on which she sat, a dresser and a buzzing contraption that seemed to emit cool air. Its run-down look was eerily similar to the tavern.

A chuckle sounded from her side. "Yeah, she's a feisty one, alright." It was the yellow-haired boy from earlier.

She cast suspicious glances at the two figures in the room with her. They looked just like the degenerates on the streets.

"Who are you people?" she asked cautiously.

"Oh, right. I guess introductions are in order. You can call me Gidget," the purple-haired girl said with a wide grin.

"Chains," the guy said casually. He had a swagger like some of the martial artists she knew back home. She must admit, he did know how to fight. She sniffed irritatingly. She hadn't forgiven him yet for calling her a helpless little girl.

"Here." He handed her a dirty vessel filled with water.

She made a face. But she realized her throat was dry as a desert and drank it all in one gulp.

"Man, being tasered is no fun. You're one tough cookie," said Gidget, her eyes wide with curiosity beneath her glasses.

"Tasered?" Jinlei frowned. "You mean that thing? With the buzzing?" She winced, recalling how it felt like her whole body was on fire. Some of the burning sensation still lingered. Plus, the throbbing pain in her head ever since she arrived in this world. She suddenly felt woozy all over again.

A strong hand supported her back. "Easy there," Chains said, taking the vessel from her.

"Where'd you learn to fight like that?" he asked.

"And what's with the funky clothes?" asked Gidget.

Jinlei studied them both carefully. Before she revealed anything, she wanted to make sure she could trust them.

"How did I get here?"

Gidget frowned as if she was insulted. "What'd you think? We rescued you."

"But why?" Jinlei shook her head to clear it. Since arriving in this world, she had only met with hostile glances her way. It was refreshing to meet somewhat friendly faces. Still, she was in unfamiliar territory. She didn't know who these people were and whether they could be trusted.

Gidget and Chains looked at each other and shrugged.

Chains shrugged. "Don't really know. We just kinda acted on it, you know? Besides, it's about time someone stood up to Snakeskin."

"Yeah," Gidget agreed thoughtfully. "Anyway, it's no fun being out on your own. We know what that's like."

Jinlei drank more water from the vessel as she surreptitiously studied the two of them. The purple-haired girl was small and probably looked younger than her actual age. Jinlei wasn't worried about her, though Jinlei could tell that, if pushed, the girl probably had a few tricks up her sleeve to survive. If anyone was a threat, it would be the yellow-haired boy with the impeccable fighting skills. But upon closer look, the boy had a nonchalance that put Jinlei at ease. Though he was rough-looking and unrefined with the way he spoke and swaggered as he walked, she felt that his lack of sophistication and unpretentiousness made him a reliable companion to the purple-haired girl.

"Have you two known each other long?" Jinlei asked, testing her theory.

Gidget rolled her eyes. "Way too long"

"Really?" Jinlei's eyebrows crinkled uncertainly.

Gidget quickly waved her hands to reassure Jinlei. "That was a joke. I meant that in the best way possible."

"Gee, thanks," Chains said drily.

"Truth is," Gidget said sincerely, "this guy saved me a few times too."

"Really?" This time, Jinlei's eyebrows arched in interest.

Gidget smiled, her eyes disappearing into half-moons. "I was bullied a lot as you can probably tell," she said somewhat bashfully.

"He always stood up for me. That's how he got so good at fighting. It's been . . . what, five years now? He's practically my big brother."

Chains scoffed and looked away, not wanting to claim the compliment but not denying it either. The perfect blend of pride and self-effacement typical of the martial artists Jinlei knew.

Jinlei relaxed, her suspicions eased. It looked like the boy, Chains, had some honor as a fighter, and the girl, Gidget, had loyalty as a friend—both necessary qualities in the code of *xia*—the martial code of honor. It looked like she could trust them after all. Taking another look at them, she realized they were just like her. All alone in this strange world.

"Thank you," she said sincerely. "I must admit—I owe you my life."

"Hey, it ain't that deep!" Gidget protested.

Jinlei shook her head. "No, really. I don't know what I would have done if I had gotten captured. Especially here, in this whole new world . . ." she trailed off, forcing back her tears. Her new reality and thoughts of her family back home came rushing to her all at once. Oh, how she hoped they were alright. She should be back home, lending her strength and helping them fight the great evil that descended upon their village. Instead, she was here, in a strange land with strange people. Somehow safe but still in a precarious situation. She hit the mattress she sat on in frustration.

"Hey," Gidget said gently, laying a sympathetic hand on her shoulder. "It's going to be okay."

"No, it's not," Jinlei objected, tears threatening to fall from her eyes. "I shouldn't be here. I have to go back home."

"Okay, then. Where's home?"

Jinlei breathed shakily. "The past. To the thirty-eighth year of Emperor Xuanzong's rule."

Gidget and Chains shared a look between them. Perhaps they thought she was crazy. Perhaps they thought she might be more dangerous than they had initially believed. But any thoughts they had were overcome by a more enticing lure—morbid curiosity.

Chains shifted to a more comfortable position. "Okay, then. Start from the beginning."

Part II
My Life as Jinlei

IV

From a young age, I was allowed to run around and play free like a boy. After having me, my mother was unable to bear any more children. I was my parents' sole child and heiress. And because of that, I was the recipient of much love. My parents indulged me and humored my whims and wishes. They educated me, let me learn how to read and write. And most of all, allowed me to learn martial arts to my heart's content.

You could say my family wasn't a very traditional one. I came from a long line of warriors. The Ling clan had protected our village and prefecture from outside threats for centuries. My mother came from the great clan of Hu. My great-grandfather Hu had the ear of the first Tang dynasty emperor, Emperor Gaozu himself. And when my parents wed, the Houses of Ling and Hu were united, becoming the most prominent warrior clan of Water Drop Village.

A prominent family may have its perks—I always had the prettiest dresses, the finest foods and the finest teachers anyone could ask for. But it also came with a huge burden and responsibility.

My family, you see, wasn't any ordinary warrior clan. The Ling clan were known as brave warriors on the battlefield. The Hu clan, however, were powerful shamans. When the two houses united, both clans doubled their strength, fighting against human and non-human threats. The Ling-Hu clan was always called upon to solve all kinds of problems—from catching criminals to exorcising demons that terrorized the prefecture.

My first martial operation came when I was just ten years old. It was a small job—exterminating a malevolent spirit that possessed a cat. Since then, I had started joining my family on small, not-so-dangerous operations. Slowly, I was given more and more responsibility and bigger and bigger jobs. And it was this last operation, which my family didn't want me involved, that was also the biggest and most dangerous. But it's precisely for that reason that I must go back home to help them.

V

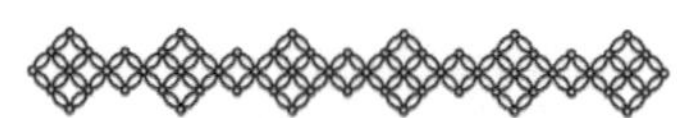

The trouble started when my family was called upon to investigate a ghost that was haunting a rich merchant's silk and spices shop in the district. Merchant Huang suspected that his business rival had plotted to curse his shop and scare customers away. We were offered a handsome sum because he couldn't afford to lose another day of business and wanted to be rid of the problem as soon as possible.

Cases like these, in which the problem involved both supernatural and human mischief, people often sought the Ling family's unique skill sets in fighting and shamanism. It was the perfect case for my childhood friend, Li Jun, and me. We often took on cases together for our families were extremely close, and we worked very well together. Jun was an expert of the Northern Dragon Style kung-fu, while I practiced the Flying White Crane style. I was great at defensive techniques and rapid hand strikes, while he had powerful legwork and offense. In business rivalry cases like Merchant Huang's, Jun would often cover me in case any hired goons ambushed us as I worked rapidly to exorcise the supernatural entity. Together, we were known as the Flying Crane and Dragon duo.

On the day that Jun and I were supposed to get rid of the

problem, an even bigger surprise greeted us. And that surprise was Xia Chengling from the noble house of Xia from the next village over. As soon as we stepped into Merchant Huang's shop, there she was, collecting what was supposed to be our pay. I didn't sense any malevolent spirits in the shop at all. From the looks of it, she had finished the job before we could even start. She had swooped in on *our* case like a deceitful snake!

I couldn't even begin to express how absolutely livid I was. I imagined heat and smoke coming out of my ears as if I had eaten a hundred spicy chilies.

I looked at Master Huang for answers. He shrugged apologetically. "Sorry. I heard you were on another case, and Miss Xia said she could get the job done right now."

"I did have another case. But I told you I'd be able to come in time!" I protested.

He merely shrugged again. "Well, what's done is done," he proceeded to nudge us all out the door.

I gave Xia Chengling my dirtiest look.

She had the gall to smile back at me. "I just thought I'd help you out, seeing how busy you are and all. Anyway, I'll see you around, I'm sure. Bye, Jun," she said with a wave, smiling ever so sweetly. I had a mind to pluck those dimpled cheeks out of her face.

"There, there," Jun tried to console me. "You're just mad because she beat you this time when you're used to winning against her. Besides, it's not like your family needs the money."

But that wasn't it. It was the injustice of the whole thing. I would never steal a case from someone else.

"That Xia Chengling has always wanted to take what's mine. Did you see how she was smiling at you?"

Jun raised an eyebrow. "Oh, I'm yours now, am I?"

I realized just then what he thought I must have implied. Despite myself, I felt my cheeks grow hot. "N-no, that's not what I . . . I just meant she always wanted what was mine. Remember how she used to take my dolls when we were kids?"

He looked at me closely, bringing his face closer to mine. I grew uncomfortable at his intense stare. Sometimes, I just couldn't tell what he was thinking, though I've known him for ages. Every outline of his smooth features seemed to call out to me in ways it never did when we were children. His high nose, sharp chin and gentle eyes were every bit the reflection of refinement and nobility running in his blood. People always remarked how handsome he was, though I never really saw it. To me, he was always my good friend, Jun. But at this angle, I somewhat understood what everyone had been saying.

He stood so close to me that his scent almost made me dizzy. He smelled of sweet osmanthus. A succulent combination of milk and peaches, it took me back to our carefree childhood days when my family would visit his estate and we would play in his garden. He always liked to stroll among the fresh blossoms, where he watched the fishes swimming freely in the pond and where sweet osmanthus trees bloomed as abundant as the stars. That was the image of Jun I liked best: carefree and innocent. He must have been there today. Finally, he let out a big, hearty laugh.

"Relax. What are you so tense about?" he said with a devilish grin. Like Xia Chengling, he also dimpled when he smiled, though his didn't displease me as much as Xia Chengling's did.

I huffed at his teasing. I didn't appreciate him making light of the situation when I was so obviously upset!

"What am I going to tell my parents?" I dismayed.

Jun's grinning face instantly softened. "I'm sure they'll understand it wasn't your fault. Come, I'll help you explain things to them."

I forced a smile at him. "No, it's alright. I can do it myself."

"It'll be alright," he gave me a gentle pat on the shoulder. "In all the years I've known you, I've never seen your parents mete out harsh punishments. They've always been fair."

"You're right. I'm just being silly," I assured him.

I wasn't afraid of my parents' punishment. I knew they were even-minded and just. But I hated disappointing anyone, especially the ones closest to me.

What I didn't want to face was my parents' look of disappointment.

<h1 style="text-align:center">VI</h1>

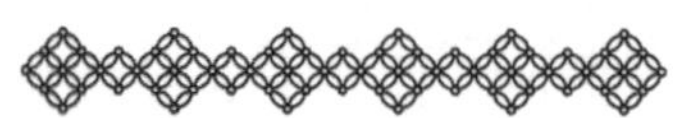

After that incident, even more troubling things happened.

The night I told my parents about Merchant Huang's case, they let me off easy, as expected. They understood it wasn't my fault. In fact, after some discussion, they came to the conclusion that it was only a matter of time that the house of Xia would have done such a thing. Xia Chengling must have been under the instruction of her parents. Our houses have been rivals for a long time. Ever since the Ling clan started gaining the favor of the governor, we became Governor Ma's preferred shamans and private handlers. It was only when we weren't available that he'd call on the house of Xia. And it wasn't exactly a secret that Xia Chengling and I had our differences. Still, I didn't think that gave her or the Xias any right to usurp our cases.

Over the next few weeks, the same thing kept happening. The Xias would beat us in solving mysterious cases—both human and supernatural. It was positively baffling since they had never been that quick before nor possessed half our skills.

I expressed to Jun how puzzled I was at the Xias' sudden rise in power. Even the governor started to call on them more often. Jun thought I was letting my rivalry with Xia Chengling cloud my better judgment. Even my parents weren't suspicious of the Xias and merely thought that we must have become complacent. My father's solution was to enforce more training on the clan. My trainings increased from twice a day—morning and night—to three times a day. Plus, surprise drills throughout the day whenever Master Fu Gong, my martial arts teacher, thought I wasn't paying attention.

Yet, no matter how hard we trained, the Xias seemed to have trained harder and continued to beat us.

On top of that, my family seemed to have run into some bad luck. Some of my parents' most trusted advisors resigned or simply disappeared and reappeared as part of the Xias' advisors or was granted official positions by the emperor himself. After that, my family was suddenly under investigation for baseless allegations of corruption and bribery. It hurt to think that my parents' most loyal counselors, whom I've thought of as my wise uncles, would betray us for no apparent reason. Even my parents were perplexed. But my father was ever the stoic pillar of our family. He took on all allegations with stride and addressed them one by one, with the help of the staff he did have left. He and his remaining loyal staff were the reason we could still hold onto our feeble position like a rapidly fraying rope. Plus, we still had the governor on our side. Until he too, was investigated for corruption and collusion with us—a potential traitor to the empire.

It all came to a head one day when Jun and I were training at my family estate's outer courtyard. Surrounding the courtyard was the receiving hall, where my father usually met with visitors, the side buildings and the gate granting entrance to the courtyard. We were practicing with wooden staffs during our sparring session. I kept going after Jun, my feet expertly going over the grey ground bricks, unaffected by its uneven surface. I struck rapidly with my staff until both our staffs broke in half.

"Alright, that's it!" Master Fu called out, a clear edge to his voice. "Miss Ling. I see your head is just not in it today."

"What do you mean?" I demanded. "I clearly won against Jun."

Master Fu's thin whiskers twitched over his frown. "This isn't about winning. It's about discipline." He tapped his staff on the ground for emphasis. "It's discipline here and here," he scolded, pointing to his head and heart. "You must learn to train your mind as well as your body. Remaining clear-headed is essential in battle. Letting your thoughts and emotions get away from yourself clouds your judgment. One wrong move and *crrrkkkk.*" He made a slicing gesture across his neck.

"Well, with the way things are going, we may as well *crrrkkk.*" I imitated his slicing motion.

Behind Master Fu, the head priest of Heaven and Earth Temple cleared his throat. Master Dao Fei had been watching our training session. He often came to visit with Mother at our family home. Our family had ties with the temple for generations, and I've known Master Dao for as long as I could remember. He was my mother's most trusted spiritual advisor and often accompanied our family on various cases. Aside from being a priest, he was also a shaman, making him one of the most powerful spiritual mediums in our region. He also performed rituals and other ceremonial duties for our family on special days such as birthdays and holidays.

"I think the child needs a break, don't you, Master Fu? The boy, too." He smiled gently.

Master Fu sniffed haughtily at Master Dao. Master Fu's harsh and disciplined demeanor contrasted with Master Dao's gentle presence.

"We still have fifteen minutes left, *Mister* Dao," Master Fu clearly dropped the Master title. I've always known that his practical nature was skeptical of spiritual occurrences and psychic phenomena, though you'd think he'd be more open-minded from being around all the mysterious, mystical events our family had had to deal with. It was only his stubbornness that kept his eyes closed to the possibilities beyond the physical world. Besides, there was always the subtle rivalry between the two masters, vying for favor within our family—the martial side and the spiritual side.

The genteel Master Dao didn't seem to mind the disrespect one bit. He was the perfect picture of Zen himself. Nothing seemed to rattle him. Hurtful words and insults just rolled off him like soft waters.

"Oh, Master Dao!" My mother emerged from the main building to the courtyard. "Here. Please bring these back with you to the temple." My mother handed Master Dao a basket of fruits, pastries, and other prepared foods. The temple survived on donations from generous patrons, of which our family made up the biggest portion.

"Ah, Lady Ling. You're too kind as always." Master Dao bowed with gratefulness.

"And *Master* Dao is right, Master Fu. The kids have had enough for today," my mother said firmly. "They are still children, after all. No need to involve them in the problems of adults for now." My mother gave me a small smile, but these past few weeks, I could tell that the small wrinkles around her eyes darkened her normally flawless face. She always kept mum around me, not wanting me to worry. *I want you to stay as my little girl for a while longer*, she told me.

Master Fu coughed, unable to counter my mother. "Very well, Lady Ling."

"It's all going to be alright, you'll see," she said for Master Fu's benefit, as well as ours.

* * *

After Master Fu somewhat eased up on our training sessions, I had more time to think and ponder about how the Xias seemed to always be one step ahead of us. I just knew in my gut something suspicious was afoot.

Whenever I asked my parents for updates about the investigations or tried to talk to them about my theories regarding the Xias, they'd always change the subject or shut down my queries. *Don't worry about it, our Little Lei. We're taking care of it*, they'd tell me. When it came down to it, they still sheltered me as if I was still a child.

I grew frustrated at the lack of information I had and the gnawing restlessness that ate up my days of feeling uncertain and knowing there must be something I could do. I knew I could help, if only my parents trusted me a bit more. I decided to take matters into my own hands.

One day I went to the town market where I knew Xia Chengling liked to shop. I spied Xia Chengling with her maidservant out on a stroll. Not wanting to miss my chance at catching them at—I wasn't sure what, but I was sure I'd find them doing something unsavory. I followed them in secret, hiding behind market stalls and people of enviable height. The hustle and bustle of the market granted me a natural cover. I always loved seeing all the colorful lanterns hanging above the streets, the variety of foods and goods, the fashionable ladies and gentlemen in their luxurious silk robes. I even loved seeing the hawkers and simple farmers whose lives must be vastly different from mine. But this was no time to dawdle about.

At one point, I was so intent on following them that I accidentally bumped into a chicken merchant. The startled chickens clucked and ca-cawed at me on top of the merchant's angry curses. The ruckus almost gave me away. I quickly hid behind a fruit stall, and they were none the wiser.

After trailing them for a while, I grew frustrated at their lack of questionable activity and almost gave up. The only questionable thing I saw was the way Miss Xia's appearance remained as fresh as the morning dew when she had been walking under the sun and crowded market as much as I have. That vexed me all the more. People told me I had a pretty moon face, but my round cheeks still reeked of childish girlhood, whereas Xia Chengling's slim face and soft features gave her the look of mature elegance. I hated to admit it, but she always carried herself with the natural poise of an accomplished young lady, while my mother still scolded me for clumsily tripping for no apparent reason or accidentally knocking something over. I couldn't help it. Sometimes I was just bursting so full of energy that I didn't know how to contain it.

I was on the verge of giving up when I spied Master Dao. I quickly hid before he could see me and say hi, so as not to inadvertently alert Xia Chengling to my presence.

But what I saw next made my heart stop. Master Dao and Xia Chengling greeted each other as if they were old friends. As far as I knew, the Xias had close ties with the Temple of Hidden Clouds. They had never set foot at 'our' temple, and we had never set foot at theirs. I steadied myself as cold dread crawled up my back when I saw them. What could they possibly be talking about?

They chatted for a while, but I wasn't close enough to hear anything they said. When they parted, I set out to trail Master Dao, heart beating quickly all the while.

I followed him all the way back to Heaven and Earth Temple. I'd been coming here since I was a child and knew every groove and crevice of the whole place. I expertly maneuvered along its hidden corners and overhanging curved eaves. Plus, it helped that the sun had gone down, and I could hide among the dark shadows.

I continued to quietly track him until I stopped just outside of what must be his personal quarters. Thankfully, one of the windows was open, presumably to let in the cool spring air. I felt uneasy peeking into his private space, but I had no choice. Fighting back a gulp, I turned my head toward the open window.

I covered my mouth with my hand to stifle a gasp.

A stench of decay and rot assaulted me through the window. There was something else—something sweet and metallic—blood? I plugged my nose and forced myself to look in closely. To say that Master Dao's living quarters were a mess was an understatement. It looked as if he hadn't tidied his room in months. There were objects strewn everywhere—books, incense, joss papers, bronze vessels used for ritualistic and ceremonial practices. But where was that stench coming from?

Master Dao proceeded to arrange four bronze altars to the north, south, east and west of the room. At the center of the altars was another bronze altar and Master Dao holding a scroll. The center altar had peculiar patterns on it that looked like horns and a mask-like appearance of a beast with no lower jaw. Years of training had heightened my spiritual sensitivity, and the center altar sent my senses ringing. It gave me a sense of foreboding, like I shouldn't be near it, much less look at it. But what could Master Dao be doing with such an item that emanated obvious malevolent energy?

He started to read from the scroll in his hands, chanting in an eerie, low voice. Soon, smoke of the color of hellish red started wafting upward from the center altar. Slowly, the smoke formed a figure resembling the theriomorphic image cast on the bronze—horns, bushy eyebrows, nose crest, ears, and a curled upper lip exposing sharp fangs but with no lower jaw.

I stifled a gasp. I now recognized the figure, which I'd seen before in those demonology books in our library. It was the face of Tao-tie—one of the four evil creatures of the world, the gluttonous beast of greed!

As the beast's smoky outline became clearer, Master Dao let out a howl of pain. A burst of energy engulfed the enclosed space within the four bronze altars. The force ripped apart Master Dao's light jacket and inner shirt. It was then that I saw the mark on his back with the same patterns as the center altar. It looked like a fresh wound, as if he had been branded by hot iron.

The mark of Tao-tie.

The foul stench of blood and rot was stronger now. It was coming from Tao-tie—the smell of decaying food and flesh.

"My lord," Master Dao uttered, kneeling before him. "You've been so good to me. Please. Tell me what else I can do for you? What can I give you?"

The red smoky outline of Tao-tie glowed brighter. "A human soul," it said as its eyes turned to look at me.

VII

I didn't know for sure if Tao-tie had seen me spying by the open window or if I had just imagined it. But I wasn't staying to find out.

I sprinted like a bolt of lightning, a silent flash in the night. I raced without stopping, my feet outpacing my heavy breaths and beating heart. The haunting image of the demon and Master Dao kept flashing in my mind like noisy fireworks. I felt the stench of blood and death on me like a curse.

I ran faster, as if I was being chased by Tao-tie and Master Dao themselves.

Past hidden alleyways, past the market, the river, until the familiar block leading back to my family home loomed in front of me. But I wasn't slowing down. One thought kept repeating in my mind: I must tell my family at once.

Finally, I reached the outer gates of my home. I banged on the closed door, yelling at the top of my lungs for them to let me in. A hand touched my shoulder. I jumped, swinging at my assailant.

My assailant blocked my strikes and finally grabbed my wrists. I resisted until a familiar voice called out to me.

"Lei-lei!" Jun brought me back to my senses. Lei-lei was the

"

name he called me since we were children.

"What happened? What's wrong?" His look of concern slowly calmed my beating heart. I glanced back to check that I wasn't indeed being chased. My racing mind slowed, and I felt safer, like I had a fighting chance if Tao-tie appeared in front of me right that second.

Just then, the large wooden doors to my home opened.

"Heavens! What is with all the noise? And at this hour," Mister Gu, my father's secretary, lightly scolded us as he ushered us in. "Your parents are waiting in the main house. They've been worried sick. You were supposed to be home before sundown. I have to call off Master Fu's little search party." He bowed as he left us, muttering to himself about having to deal with Master Fu.

Shakily, I led Jun to the main house, which housed my parents' residence. All the while, Jun kept asking me what had happened that frightened me so. My lips remained shut as I struggled in my head to make sense of what I had just seen.

When we reached the main building, my mother rushed to embrace me tightly, relieved that nothing had happened to me.

As soon as I saw my mother, I started to speak, the words rushing out of me in an incoherent babble. My mother stopped me, saying "Alright, alright. Slow down. Come. Why don't we sit a while and you can gather your thoughts. Hm?"

My mother proceeded to ask her attendants to bring out food for my supper and for our guest, Jun.

Once we've all settled around the table with plates of food and enough tea for everyone, I breathed deeply, forcing myself to remain calm, just as Master Fu had instructed. With the flashing images in my mind steadying to static images, I proceeded to tell them all that I saw about Master Dao's treachery.

When I finished, my dear mother shook her head in disbelief.

"I've known Master Dao since I was a little girl. What could possibly have possessed him to conceive of such a thing?"

"The spirit of Tao-tie, apparently," I replied wryly.

She shook her head again. "No, it sounds like he summoned Tao-tie, and now Tao-tie has him doing evil acts. So the question remains—why did he want to summon Tao-tie in the first place? And what is he planning?"

"We must act immediately," my father, who was always the voice of reason, said sternly. "First thing tomorrow, we'll invite him here. We'll pretend like we don't know a thing and get him to confess. If he doesn't—then we'll have no choice but to employ a stronger means of interrogation."

Mother gasped. "You can't possibly. He has been a friend of this family for ages and has helped us in many ways before."

Father showed no emotion but, for the sake of my mother, adopted a gentler tone. "I'm aware. That is why I'd prefer to coax it out of him rather than the other method."

"Well, we know for sure that he's decided to help the Xias behind our back, but for what reason, I don't know," I said, still feeling the chill of Tao-tie's dark energy. There were plates of dumplings, steamed fish, bamboo shoots and a bowl of piping-hot beef noodle soup in front of me, but I hadn't even picked up my chopsticks. I had no appetite to speak of.

"What sort of power does Tao-tie grant a person?" asked Jun, after swallowing a dumpling.

"It really depends on what the summoner asks for," said Mother, sipping her tea. "It could be anything from something very simple like being granted the power of gluttony—to be able to eat anything and maintain one's weight, to something more sinister like being able to eat something bigger and smarter."

Jun forced back a choke. "Bigger and smarter? You mean, feeding on humans? But for what reason?"

"Yes," Mother replied abjectly. "The power to consume one's opponent—it could be a useful skill in the battlefield."

Cold sweat erupted on my back once again. Tao-tie said it wanted a human soul. Does that mean Master Dao would be feeding it actual human beings of flesh and blood? And was that the power Master Dao asked for—to be able to consume humans himself? I tried not to wretch as the savory smells of steamed foods and hot beef broth wafted under my nose.

"Let's not jump to conclusions until we find out more." Father waved away the unpleasantness that surrounded the room. "I suggest you all get a good night's sleep."

Feeling the weariness in my bones, I knew Father was right. Tomorrow, we would need all our energy for a treacherous enemy, the likes of which we had never faced before.

VIII

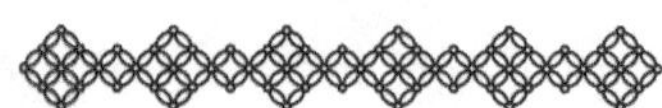

I bolted out of bed the next morning upon hearing the stealthy shuffle of feet going swiftly back and forth outside. Father must have started giving orders to capture Master Dao and bring him here. I dressed hastily, not wanting to miss anything.

I ran to the main house, where I knew Father would be holding court for the rest of the day and where he would probably be interrogating Master Dao. But I was banished as soon as I showed up at his door.

He looked up from the book he was reading when he heard me arrive. As soon as he saw me, he let out a low grumble. "This is a delicate matter, young lady. It's no place for you," he said.

I protested, "But I was the one who told you all about it in the first place! I should be allowed to interrogate him as well."

"This is a very sensitive affair. We mustn't let on what we know. As you said, you weren't sure if Tao-tie really saw you or not. If not, we still have a chance to catch Master Dao unaware. It's best if he confesses to his treachery by a slip of the tongue. And for that, it requires some delicate maneuvering. I can't have you around for any distraction."

"But—"

"Enough!" Father slammed his palm on the table as a warning. "I have to prepare myself. You may take your leave." He turned back to his table to pore over his book.

I clenched my fists as I showed myself out the door. *Fine*, I thought. But I won't be kept in the dark.

I scaled the wall outside my father's quarters and leaped to the roof. I could see all the buildings that made up our compound. From my vantage point, the curved, yellow-glazed roof tiles bordered the square courtyards and lush, landscaped garden at the rear of the compound, farthest from the main entrance. With a wide-angle view of the whole estate, I'd be able to see the moment Master Dao arrived.

I sat on the shingled rooftop for a while, pondering over and over in my head yesterday's events. Shortly, my father's secretary, with two of my father's soldiers from his army trailing behind him, walked through the main entrance gates with no Master Dao. My eyebrows furrowed with worry.

Secretary Gu was my father's right-hand man, but he was no fighter. My father must have sent him to call on Master Dao to not arouse any suspicion, and the soldiers must have been shadowing him in case there were any complications. Yet, they arrived without Master Dao. Something must have gone wrong.

I leaped down from the roof and crept along the wall toward my father's open window.

Just in time—Secretary Gu was just about to give his report. "My lord . . ."

"What's the matter?" My father was still calm, but I detected a note of alarm in his voice.

"He wasn't there when I got to the temple. I asked the temple acolytes if they knew of his whereabouts, and no one knew where he was. I asked around town as well. It's strange, but he's nowhere to be found. Usually, his closest disciples would know his plans or go with him to his obligations, but even they didn't know where he had gone. They thought it strange as well."

Father slapped his knee in frustration. "He must know we're onto him. Or he must have something big planned. Alright." He scratched his beard, the wheels in his head clearly turning out a plan. "Spread some of our soldiers and police throughout the village, but keep it quiet. Ten should do. Ask them to wear regular clothes and go on as if they were just mingling about town. But ask them to report back anything they find unusual and find out what Master Dao is up to. Remember—keep it quiet. If any trouble arises, they'll also be the first line of defense, but at least one of them should make their way back here to report back to us. As for the rest, ask them to be ready. They could be called on anytime. Ten armed soldiers should be posted here, at the estate. Ten should be ready to be deployed around the village entrance. The rest around the village square."

"Understood, sir." Secretary Gu nodded.

"The ten armed soldiers should be here as soon as possible. But be discreet."

"Right away, sir." With a bow, Secretary Gu hastened to enact my father's instructions.

I slumped against the wall. What could be happening? My stomach started to churn and croak as if a frog were leaping inside it. I couldn't stand just anxiously waiting around, so I made my way to our family's training hall.

I grabbed my favorite weapon—the bladed fans. My father had these specially made for me in the design I liked, in the color of blush. I practiced for hours until I exhausted myself.

By dusk, there was still no news of Master Dao nor from our spies around the village. Everything seemed normal. Perhaps there really was nothing to be concerned about. I started questioning what I saw yesterday. Perhaps the heat and tiredness from a day of spying on Xia Chengling made me hallucinate visions of Tao-tie? I wiped the sweat off my forehead. No, I know what I saw.

I made my way out of the training hall to ask my attendant for a snack when I sensed a shift in the air. A drum beat in the distance, a signal to deploy the soldiers. One of my father's spies burst through the main gates, shouting, "Help! Help!"

My father rushed out from his quarters in his full armor, my mother and I not far behind.

"What happened?" Father demanded.

In between gulps of breaths, the spy managed to churn out, "*Jiangshi*—reanimated corpses . . . out in the town . . ."

Mother's hand flew to her mouth in shock.

Father drew his sword. "Alright, men! Defend our people! Remember, the jiangshi can be killed by beheading."

"How many are there?" Mother asked.

"There must be over a hundred of them," the spy replied breathlessly.

"That must be Master Dao's doing," Mother turned to Father. "No one else could possibly be powerful enough to reanimate that many corpses at the same time."

"Not only that . . ." the spy continued, catching his breath. "The Xia army is also on the move."

"What?!" Father demanded angrily. "Where is the governor?"

"I heard from another spy—the Xia army and the jiangshi easily took down the governor and his staff as they were caught unaware.

Besides, it looks like Governor Ma's police chief betrayed him. Officer Zuo turned Governor Ma's own police officers and military personnel against him, then Officer Zuo himself killed Governor Ma. And now, the governor's troops have joined the Xias."

Father cursed loudly. "We were playing it too safe, trying to silently stalk Master Dao like a tiger in the grass. In truth, we were nothing but a kitten! I should have warned Governor Ma."

"You couldn't have known." Mother went over to Father and gently touched his arm.

"We're just a little ahead of the enemy," the spy reassured us. "We're more prepared than the governor, and our soldiers have been deployed. However, the enemy is on their way here."

"You did well, young lad. When all this is over, come find me, and I will personally thank you."

The spy's eyes glistened with surprise and gratitude. He bowed ardently. "Thank you. I'm of service to you, my lord."

Father turned to Mother and me and whispered so that only we could hear, "Go to the servants' quarters and hide there. No one will think to look for you there."

"Father!" I started to protest.

He interrupted me with a loud, angry voice and a red fury in his eyes that I had never seen before. "Don't be foolish, Jinlei! For once, just do as I say!" He coldly dismissed me as he turned back toward his troops, his armor clanking away from us.

"Come, Jinlei!" my mother urged, pulling my arm as we hastened over to the servants' quarters.

The servants led us to the kitchen storehouse. It was filled with jars of fermented foods, wine and shelves full of stored food and kitchen tools. We hid behind the tall sacks of rice. Outside, we could hear the commotion. The enemy soldiers and the jiangshi must have made it past our gates. We kept silent, clinging to each other, hoping that it would all be over soon.

Before long, the screams and clamor could be heard just outside the storehouse. There was no way the enemy could find us here, I tried to reassure myself.

The door slammed open, and the sound of slow, heavy footsteps came in, then stopped. Mother and I held our breaths. *Please let him leave soon*, I prayed silently.

"Come out, come out! I know you're here!"

That voice. My eyes widened, and I saw my mother's expression mirror my own. We would know that slightly nasal pitch anywhere, though it was now devoid of the serene touch we were used to. Instead, the voice carried a mocking, contemptuous note. It was Master Dao.

He kicked a shelf to make a loud banging noise. "Come now. I sensed your nervous *qi*—your energetic life force—from outside. I know you're in here."

I tightened my fist. Mother and I had tried to hide our qi, our energy. The qi we emitted must have been the size of a tiny mouse, at best. If Master Dao could sense that, then in such a short time, he must have become a lot more powerful than I had thought.

He kicked a shelf again, rattling the contents on it. It sounded like vases were about to topple and break but didn't.

"Either you reveal yourselves, or I make you reveal yourselves!"

Before I could stop her, Mother stood up to face Master Dao. "It's just me," she said.

Master Dao scoffed. "Don't insult me, Lady Ling. I know Miss Jinlei's with you."

Before my mother could stop me, I stood up as well. As soon as Master Dao's face was in my full view, I almost doubled over in shock. It wasn't only his voice that had changed but his whole person. It looked like he was even taller than before. His white-bearded face still had the semblance of the old Master Dao, though it had taken on a more grotesque look. His eyes were beadier, his nose was more crooked and his cheeks were swollen as if he had been punched a hundred times. His body bulged in all the wrong places as if he had eaten too much, and the excess portions were mindlessly stuffed where there was room. How could someone have changed so much overnight? The thought gave me a shudder. Was that what the power of Tao-tie granted him? He was so swollen because he had eaten too much? And what did he eat? I'd rather not know.

Mother said out loud what I had no courage to say. "Master Dao . . . why . . . What happened to you?"

He seemed to take offense at our shock as his beady eyes narrowed at us, but at the same time seemed amused as his mustache curled upward in a sneer.

"Why, Lady Ling, is that any way to greet an old friend?"

"You're nothing like my old friend at all!" Mother spat back. "Even your qi's different. It's something vile . . . something not of this world . . ."

Master Dao laughed heartily, like he was pleased by my mother's words. "Well, you're right about that, Lady Ling. I'm not like 'your old friend' at all—that spineless, pathetic, weak old man. I've been given a new life. New strength! As for my qi—well, that's just a natural consequence of my newfound power."

"But *why*, Master Dao?" Mother's voice filled with regret and deep sadness. "You have always been powerful. You've helped us on so many cases, fought alongside us to exorcise some of the vilest creatures and malevolent spirits out there!"

Master Dao's qi suddenly flared up in rage, his bright red aura almost blinding me. "Apparently not powerful enough!"

"You were!" Mother insisted. "We . . . no, *I* couldn't have asked for a better priest, nor a better friend!"

Master Dao's aura subsided, but the anger and contempt remained. He managed to keep his aura under control to a steady hum of pulsing intensity. "A friend, am I? And yet, I still suffered your betrayal."

Mother and I looked at each other in confusion. "What betrayal?" Mother asked.

Master Dao's aura flared up again. "Don't pretend! Well, no matter. You'll get what you deserve!"

Master Dao reached to his side as if drawing a sword, then thrust his palms forward and released an energy blast that looked like a red fireball with horns, bushy eyebrows and sharp fangs with no lower jaw—the figure of Tao-tie. I instinctively shoved my mother out of the way, and I bounded to the other side.

We both barely missed it, but it got my left arm and my mother's right. I grabbed my left arm, trying to squeeze the pain away. For a while, my left arm couldn't move, as if the energy had been sucked out of it.

Mother gasped. "So that's what you asked for? For Tao-tie to give you the power to consume souls?"

"Not souls—qi. The more qi I consume, the more powerful I become and the weaker my opponent gets. As you know, qi can get replenished after some rest, recovery and qi cultivation practices. Souls—you can never get back. I must admit, consuming souls might have been a better deal. But I asked Tao-tie for the power to aid me in battle, and this is what he gave me. It's powerful enough, if I must say so myself."

"And what did you have to give up to get that power?" I demanded, recalling Tao-tie's desire for a human soul.

"Good question. You were always an astute student, young Jinlei. It was the usual blood contract."

My mother's eyes narrowed in suspicion. "For a power like that and for you to be able to reanimate a hundred corpses, it wasn't just a regular blood contract, was it?"

"Right you are, Mistress Ling. Your daughter really does take after you. I had to give it a hundred blood contracts. A hundred souls in exchange for all the money, power and fame a person desires."

"So the Xias and Governor Ma's chief of police . . ." I started, uttering in disbelief.

Master Dao's whiskers twitched with pleasure. ". . . were all too willing to join me. They were tired of the status quo, of the select few who hold onto power and enrich themselves, while the rest of us scramble after scraps. They were only too eager to give up their souls in exchange for Tao-tie's promised gifts."

Mother gave out a pained cry, not out of physical pain, but out of Master Dao's perception of our family. I understood the pain behind Mother's lamentation. We had been friends for so long. How could he think all that we did was for the selfish gain of power and wealth? Or did he covet power so much that it corrupted his judgment?

"How could you punish us for holding onto power when you desire power for yourself?" I sputtered incredulously.

"The difference between your family and me is that I'm at least honest about my intentions. Just like I am with this! Hyah!" He sent double energy blasts to me and Mother. We both expertly dodged out of the way.

I took out my fans, and Mother unsheathed her weapon of choice—the sword of heaven, a longsword with inscriptions of holy sutras on its blade, meant to purify any evil entity it touched. It was the perfect weapon with which to combat Master Dao.

Mother went first, holding the hilt with both hands, poised by her temple in a jabbing position. She jabbed and sliced across, while I moved to Master Dao's rear to strike. Despite his heavier frame, he moved swift and lithe, parrying and repelling our attacks. Master Dao was never much of a fighter, but it was evident that Tao-tie had granted him increased speed and strength with a formidable onslaught of martial arts knowledge.

He moved big, with big arm and leg swings that moved in a crushing motion. Mother was relentless, matching his big moves with her longsword. She cut and sliced at his open stances, but he somehow always managed to close the gap and nimbly steer clear of Mother's blades and mine. The storehouse was quite narrow and we couldn't help but knock down the shelves and vases stored with foodstuffs. At one point, Mother accidentally sliced open a sack of rice. Pretty soon, the floor of the cramped space filled up with all kinds of dried food, pickled juices, and produce hacked to pieces. In situations like these, a mere slip of the foot could be the difference between life and death.

I tried not to lose my footing as I dashed and jumped on top of the slippery floor filled with spilled juices and food scraps. His arm arched toward my shoulder. I crossed my arms in a block, catching his arm between mine. I twisted my arms to catch his in a lock, but he cross-maneuvered and caught my arms in a twist. In one swift move, he had me in a bear hug and turned me toward Mother. Mother's blade came speeding at me, and I didn't have time to yell.

In that split second, I thought how ill-fated was I to die by my own mother's hand. But she stopped her blade in time, within inches of my face. I felt myself being thrown forward and Mother catching me fervently. In that quick instant, I felt her intense relief at holding my living body.

Perhaps we held onto each other for a second too long because it gave Master Dao just enough time to unleash another energy blast, hitting us both. The red heat engulfed my whole body and I felt the strength draining from me. I became dizzy and light-headed, my legs buckling, my own feet not able to hold me up. Mother and I gave in to the slippery floor and crashed weakly to the ground.

Master Dao towered over us, a look of triumph on his face as he prepared his finishing move. He held his palms in front of him and, in my dizzied state, saw the swirl of red energy gather into the palms of one Master Dao.

The sound of frenzied footsteps behind him made him stop and whirl around, narrowly missing the slice of Jun's dragon saber.

"Auntie! Jinlei! Go now! Leave him to me!" he called out between attacks.

My whole body felt like heavy lead, yet we weren't done, Mother and I. There was no way we would leave Jun behind. We pushed ourselves off the floor with our sheer force of will rather than strength. Despite the damage we undertook, we still had a little more fight in us. Mother's blade must have protected us somewhat, for she held it in front of us when we received the blow. It was the first point of contact against Master Dao's energy blast, thereby absorbing some of its damage.

To my surprise, Mother dropped her sword and started to do slow arm and hand movements. I couldn't hear what she was saying, but she was chanting something as she was doing the fluid motions with her hands and legs. My mother practiced tai chi but this form was nothing I had ever seen before.

While my mother was in a trance, Master Dao tried to unleash another energy blast, but I tackled him at the same time that Jun unleashed his sword. Master Dao twisted his body, maneuvering both of us away from Jun's sword. He shoved me aside, taking a piece of broken glass, and tussled with Jun. He managed to inflict small slices upon Jun's skin, little pools of blood wetting his clothes. All the while, he made sure I was behind him, protecting me.

Soon, a majestic, swirling vortex opened up in front of us. It looked like a small universe had emerged, filled with stars and light and pure energy—the time portal.

"Quick, Jinlei! Get in!" Mother urged me, pushing me toward the portal.

"Ma!" I called out to her, trying to pull her in with me, but she pushed as hard as I pulled.

"Ma! I won't leave you!" I objected desperately as tears started streaming down my face.

In the end, I couldn't win against the strength of years she had over me as she pushed me all the way in, her fingers slipping from mine.

That was the last I saw of my mother and Jun.

Part III

IX

"So that's why you reek like rotten garbage," Chains uttered absent-mindedly, his eyes glazed over like a fool.

"Excuse me?" Jinlei demanded. Still, she sniffed herself. She smelled of dried, pickled juice. She wrinkled her nose and had a mind to slap Chains for the insult. But his remark briefly took her mind off the tearful parting with her mother, and for that, she was grateful.

Gidget just stared at them open-mouthed. Chains nudged her, and she came to her senses. "So . . . time travel, huh?" She scanned Jinlei from head to toe, fixing her glasses properly so she could see better. "Kind of a tall tale, don't you think?"

Jinlei's shoulders deflated. Even she couldn't deny how far-fetched her tale sounded. But she had no other means of defending herself, except to insist upon its truth. "I know it's hard to believe. But I do not know what else to tell you. I could hardly believe the whole thing myself, except that I'm right here in front of you, seeing and feeling this strange world and all its confounding apparatuses."

Chains scratched his head anxiously. "I mean she definitely doesn't sound like she's from our time," he offered to Gidget.

Gidget shrugged. "Well, for a tech geek like me, I do love tall tales like this." She chuckled incredulously. "Man . . . time travel. Even with our advanced technology, we still haven't figured out a way to bridge the space-time continuum. I can't believe Ancient China had it figured out. I guess we could learn a thing or two from you." She paused thoughtfully. "So all you have to do is open the time portal like your mom did, right?"

Jinlei's shoulders sagged. "Yes, but I don't know how. She never taught me. It's a very advanced spell, passed down the Hu line—my mother's ancestral line. I wouldn't have been allowed to learn it until I've passed a series of tests to prove I was capable enough."

Gidget mirrored Jinlei's disappointment. "So you're stuck here then? Is there a way to find your mother's spell? But you saw the hand movements she did. Do you remember how to do them?"

Jinlei nodded. "Yes, I seem to recall what she did, though I was in a weakened state and my mind was in a fog, so I can't be completely confident that I remember exactly. Besides, without the spoken spell, the tai chi movements aren't enough."

"Let's ask the Omniscience," said Gidget.

Jinlei crinkled her eyebrows questioningly.

Gidget took out a small device and talked into it. "Hey, Omni. What's the tai chi spell to time travel?"

To Jinlei's amazement, the device spoke back.

"Interesting question! While I don't have direct knowledge of ancient tai chi spells for time travel, it seems this is something tied more closely to mystical traditions or forgotten knowledge. Tai chi is about balance, energy . . ."

Gidget sighed, swiping the device with her thumb in an upward motion. "Figures there wouldn't be anything."

"What is that thing? It can talk to you?" Jinlei peered at it in wonder.

"Oh, this? Yeah, it's a phone and an encyclopedia and a map and . . . I'll explain to you later," Gidget smiled nonchalantly upon seeing Jinlei's bewildered face. "Anyway, do you have any other ideas on how to figure out the spell?"

Jinlei nodded. "My mother's family kept extensive records. It must be at our old home in our village."

Chains punched the air enthusiastically. "Alright! To Jinlei's village we go!"

Jinlei blinked, holding back the onset of tears that threatened to roll down her tired eyes. She couldn't believe they were so willing to help her when they were mere strangers just a few hours ago.

"Hey, uh . . . it's no big deal, you know? We got nothing else anyway," Chains said quickly upon noticing Jinlei's teary eyes. He was clearly uncomfortable at her overwhelming emotions.

"Yeah," Gidget added, trying to comfort her. "Honestly, we drift here and there, taking up odd jobs when and where we can. There are not much opportunities for people like us when you don't have the right family background or connections. This whole country is built on nepotism and patronage. There's no hope for us. We're like ghosts in this city."

"That's why choosing between fighting a dog for a bone and a new adventure—it's really a no-brainer." Chains grinned, sticking his thumb up.

"I see." Jinlei softened at them upon hearing their hardships. "I'm sorry to hear that, but I'm grateful for your company." She smiled. "I'll be sure to pay you back the favor somehow."

Chains waved a hand dismissively. "So, where is this village of yours?"

"Just on the outskirts of Chang'an. It shouldn't take more than a few days by horse."

Chains and Gidget stifled a giggle.

"Stick with us, kid, and we'll show you how the world works," said Chains with an impish grin.

X

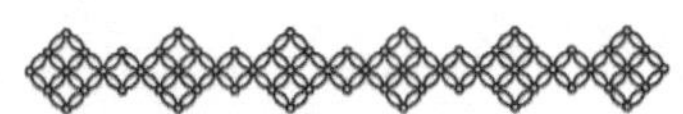

The next day, Chains and Gidget took Jinlei to the heart of Chang'an to take the train to Water Drop Village.

Jinlei marveled at the sky-piercing concrete buildings with moving pictures on them. Chains and Gidget explained to her what televisions and screens were. She still didn't get it, but she thought that the future had very advanced magic.

She couldn't keep her head down while walking as she gazed with open-mouthed attention at the flashy city, making her bump into a few people who yelled curses at her. Others stopped and stared when they saw her old-fashioned robes and elegant accessories. They probably wondered if she had on real jewels.

"Erm—" Gidget gently steered Jinlei to the inside of the sidewalk. "We can't keep going on like this. She's attracting too much attention."

"You're right," Chains agreed.

Gidget nodded to a side street. "Let's go in there," she said, taking Jinlei's arm.

"Hey, what? Where?" Jinlei finally snapped out of it.

"We're going to do a little shopping." Gidget grinned.

The shops on the side streets weren't as flashy as the ones on the main shopping plaza. Here, the shops were darker. Smaller. Grimier. There were more shops and people than seemed necessary for a small street. Jinlei felt all eyes on her, drinking her in as if she were cheap wine. She self-consciously shrunk back. Why do people in the future keep staring at her?

Gidget pulled her into a shop. "Here."

The shop was a small square room, each side about as long as her and Chains's arms spread wide open. But the shop made full use of the space by cramming it full of racks and racks of clothes.

Gidget started picking out clothes and held them up against Jinlei to see how they might look on her.

Jinlei made a face. She had no intention of wearing shiny black cowhides. Besides, they looked very stiff and uncomfortable. She wondered how Chains could move so fluidly in his tight pants.

"How 'bout these?" Chains picked up some bright-colored clothes that seemed to glow despite the dim interior.

Jinlei cocked her head to the side to examine them. They were a little better, but she thought the bright colors might still catch too much attention. She walked over to another rack, with clothes made of simple cotton material, in neutral colors like black, gray, and dark green. She pointed to them. "These," she simply said.

Chains nodded. "Simple. I like it."

Jinlei smiled with satisfaction. She picked out a gray tank top, a black jacket, fatigue pants, black boots and a navy green cap. The sleepy store clerk pointed lazily to a curtained room, where Jinlei went to try on the clothes.

When she emerged with her new clothes, Gidget and Chains nodded their approval. Jinlei picked out a few more extra clothes and a backpack like the ones Chains and Gidget had to put everything in.

Gidget handed over the money to the store clerk.

Jinlei bit her lip. "I'm sorry for your trouble. Maybe there's a way I can pay you back?"

"Hey, don't worry about it," Gidget said as she worriedly stared at the dwindling cash in her wallet. "I mean, you just arrived. It's not like you'd have any money anyway."

"Well . . ." Jinlei began before cutting herself off as she noticed the store clerk eye them curiously. She led them both to a more private corner outside. "My jewels . . ."

Chains and Gidget exchanged a look. Jinlei knew they must have noticed her jewels earlier but were too kind-hearted to have said anything.

"Perhaps we can exchange them for money?"

Chains and Gidget both gulped at the thought.

"A-are you sure?" asked Chains.

It was the first time Jinlei had seen him flustered. "But whyever not? Well? Shall we get on with it?" It was the least she could do for all the help she had received from them.

"Yeah . . ." Gidget started. "There's a pawnshop this way."

They arrived at a stall with a little man inside a cage, counting money.

"Sir," Gidget called to him. He looked at them with the same blank eyes as everyone on the street. "We have something we need assessed."

The little man grunted his acknowledgment. Gidget rolled her eyes as Jinlei surreptitiously took out a necklace, trying not to attract attention. The little man's eyes grew wider and the blank look seemed to disappear as he took out a device which he put on his eye to examine the jewelry.

The little man assessed it carefully and gave a little cough. Jinlei could tell that he tried to hide his excitement. When he was finished, he declared with a straight face, "Right. I can give you three thousand yuan for this."

"What?" Gidget demanded. "That's gotta be worth at least fourteen thousand," she said through gritted teeth, trying not to make a scene.

The little man scoffed. "You flatter yourself, little lady. Sure, this is a good piece, but it ain't that good. See the scratch marks here?"

"You can barely see it," Gidget protested.

"That's the best I can do," the little man said, raising his hands up. "You won't get a better deal than this. Do you think anybody else here can afford to give you fourteen thousand yuan?" He scoffed.

Chains went up to the cage, dangerously eclipsing the little man.

But the little man was unperturbed. He was safe inside his cage, after all. "Well? Come and get me, big boy. If you can." He laughed tauntingly.

Jinlei grabbed Gidget's arm, urging them not to cause any more trouble. "Let's go. Let's just find someone else."

"You're not going to find anyone better, missy." The little man crossed his arms smugly.

"We'll see about that," Gidget huffed.

She was about to grab the necklace back, but the little man quickly pulled it away from her. There was no way any of them could reach inside the bars. The little man held it up in front of them with an amused sneer.

"Give it back," Gidget hissed.

"You know you really should show better respect to your elders. You should have just taken the offer I gave you. It was a generous one at that," he said, pocketing the necklace.

Chains banged on the cage bars, trying to rattle it open. Passersby stopped and looked. The little man didn't like this and started to shout.

"Stop disturbing my business, you spoiled brats! You probably stole this anyway. Now scram!" He reached up the cage bars to bring down the shutters, but that made him close enough for Chains to reach in between the bars to grab him.

Chains pulled on his collar, pressing his face against the bars. The little man's face turned a crimson purple as he choked, gasping for air.

Chains said in a low, dangerous voice, "Hand it over, little man." Chains tightened his grasp on the little man.

The little man reached in his pocket, feeling for the necklace and handed it over to Chains with shaky hands.

Chains let go, and the little man coughed violently as he gently rubbed his neck.

The trio was about to leave when the little man called out, "Wait! I'll give you ten thousand for it."

Chains slammed a fist against the cage. The little man jumped and cowered a little but insisted, "That's the best I can do. You won't find a better offer anywhere else." When he sensed that the trio were still not convinced, he added, "Come on, look around you. You think anybody here has that much cash?" His voice started rising, along with his anger all over again.

Jinlei nudged them both. "Let's just take it," she said, suddenly feeling sorry for the little man.

"Fine," Chains sighed.

Gidget gave the little man the necklace and gingerly put the money in her backpack. They agreed Gidget would handle the cash since Jinlei wasn't familiar with how things worked in the modern world.

When they were well out of the little man's sight, Jinlei lightly scolded Chains. "You were too rough on him."

He scoffed. "Open your eyes, princess. That's the way things are done here. Besides, he was all too willing to take us for a ride."

Jinlei frowned. "Still. He was an old man."

Chains suddenly stopped and turned to face Jinlei. "I wasn't really going to hurt him," he said defensively. "Out here, you have to show strength, or you'll get eaten up alive. Besides, these guys are usually backed by gangsters. He would have fed us to the wolves—vicious criminals that make Snakeskin look like a fluffy bunny."

Jinlei felt a red flush rush to her face. She didn't like to be told when she was wrong. Even worse, she didn't like it when she was actually wrong. But Chains was wrong too. It wasn't fair for someone like him to impress his strength upon an obviously feeble man.

"And what if he wasn't backed by gangsters? Then you would have dishonorably ganged up on a poor old man."

"Dishonorable?" Chains looked at her wide-eyed, then scoffed again. He couldn't believe what he was hearing. "Listen, you . . ."

"Hey, hey . . ." Gidget put herself in between the two. "Do we really have to fight about this? Jinlei, Chains is right. You don't know this, but this area is a hotbed of criminal activity. Why do you think everything's so cheap? Everything you bought today—your whole outfit and your backpack only cost one hundred yuan. That's because everything here is bootleg, sometimes stolen," Gidget explained in a hushed tone.

Jinlei's face reddened even more. She despised not knowing anything. Back home, even though her parents allowed her certain liberties, they always tried to protect her from heavier burdens. Therefore, she was often kept in the dark. But she had ways of skirting around her parents' rules and roaming about town. Back home, everything was clear. She was certain of her place in society, confident in her knowledge of the world she lived in. Out here—now—she felt all alone amidst a cruel sea, balancing on a wooden plank with one leg, unsure if she would fall in or not. She balled her hands into fists.

"Come on," Gidget prodded gently. "We still have a train to catch. Besides, thanks to Chains, we have enough money for travel."

Jinlei took a deep breath. Gidget was right. And the sooner she can go back home, the sooner she can leave this place and help her family. She nodded to Chains by way of apology, not quite meeting his eyes. Chains merely grunted.

They made their way back toward the main shopping street. Jinlei felt more comfortable as she blended in with the crowd. No more uneasy stares. Now, she can freely take in her surroundings. Too many things demanded her attention at once as the shining modern city continuously blinked at her. It was curious.

Despite all the bright lights and glare from flashing screens, the city itself seemed dark and bleak, as if the tall buildings blocked out the sky and the sun. The sun here wasn't as bright as the sun back home. The air wasn't as fresh either. In this world, the air seemed to choke you with smoke and rotten garbage. Back home, the open air reflected the seasons—the flowery springs, the sweaty summers, the leafy autumns and the frosty winters.

The building facades showed images on their screens of pristine-looking ladies and gentlemen instructing people how to wash their faces and hair. Jinlei watched with rapt interest. Apparently, in the future, they've developed ways to preserve youth and beauty. She may have to stock up on such supplies before her trip back home.

They arrived at the main public square, stretching almost as wide as the sea. People seemed to gather here for many reasons. Music blasted from somewhere and some people were dancing as a small crowd gathered around them. Some casually strolled around, some practiced outdoor tai chi and others came by to see the Daming Palace from a distance. Just ahead was the Danfeng Gate, the main entrance to the palace, which was reliably closed to the public. High concrete walls surrounded the whole palace complex. The curved roofs of the Daming Palace, the emperor's imperial residence, loomed behind the walls just as majestically as Jinlei had remembered it. She had taken a trip to the imperial capital once or twice before. She loved coming to the big city and marveled at the busy metropolis with its market districts, Silk Road merchants, and tall pagodas, so different from her peaceful village. She never imagined the future consisted of tall blocks of miserable, gray concrete that overpowered nature itself. It was completely unrecognizable, save for the palace complex.

"I'm glad a piece of our heritage wasn't lost, at least," she murmured to herself, not intending her thoughts to be heard.

"Yeah, well. Only the chosen few get to live in the palace," Gidget responded to her thoughts.

Jinlei figured some things just didn't change. "It was the same back home. Only the royal family and their staff lived in the palace."

"Well, now it's the president of the country, the state council, and pretty much Corp. X," Chains chimed in.

"Corp. X?" echoed Jinlei.

They walked closer to the Danfeng Gate, guarded by a row of guards. Chains nodded to the massive, sleek, pearly white structure that towered beyond the gate, dominating the skyline. It stood taller and shone brighter than all the other buildings, even overshadowing the palace itself.

"Corporation X—the most powerful and richest corporation in the world. They produce the most innovative technology out there, and they have a hand in every pie, from robotics, biotech, phones, cars, artificial intelligence, you name it," Gidget explained.

"And they work hand-in-hand with the government. The government helps fund their programs, and they help fund the government. It's a vicious cycle of them enriching each other while the rest of us fight to the death just to earn a few hundred yuan. They even built their headquarters right next to the palace just to rub it in our faces." Chains spit on the ground in disgust.

The little hairs on Jinlei's back stood up. She was on high alert with all the security personnel around her. Around the city and especially around the palace, she had noticed what she assumed to be armed soldiers walking around the city in their modern armor and weapons. Their armors weren't made of metal. Chains said they were made of advanced, reactive alloy and smart fabrics, and the long weapons were called 'laser rifles.' They were clad in shades of green and brown, and the material looked sturdier than the metal plates back home.

There were also other security personnel clad in similar armor but were all in black.

"Those are Corp. X's soldiers, the ones in black," Chains pointed out. "There must be some Corp. X big wigs in the palace now, probably some important meeting with the government."

Jinlei got a strange feeling watching Corp. X's security personnel. She sensed that Corp. X's soldiers were of a different caliber altogether.

"Should Corp. X's soldiers be more powerful than the government's own soldiers?" Jinlei asked.

Chains regarded her curiously. "Why would you say that? The government troops are more powerful, of course. Corp. X's soldiers have never been in an actual war."

Jinlei chewed thoughtfully on her lip. Having been trained in the internal spiritual arts granted her a higher sensitivity than most. She couldn't shake the uneasy feeling she got from Corp. X's troops. "You may be right. It's just that I have a feeling that their armor seems to hide more than it protects. Whatever it's hiding can't be good."

Chains rubbed his chin, considering Jinlei's thoughts. "Well, whatever it is, I wouldn't put it past Corp. X. They're capable of a lot of things we can't even imagine."

Jinlei's heart stopped as the giant screen on Corp. X's façade changed to a portrait of a familiar face, except she wore a modern, shoulder-length hairstyle and a modern, white immaculate suit.

"Xia Chengling," she gasped.

Gidget turned toward her in surprise. "You mean that lady? No, that's Xia Chiling, the daughter of Corp. X's aging patriarch. That one's her brother, Xia Cheng-cheng. One of them is slated to take over from the elder Xia when he steps down . . . or dies."

Jinlei couldn't believe it. The lady on the screen was the spitting image of Xia Chengling. She couldn't have survived all this time, could she? No. That was impossible. Still . . . Jinlei was sent to the future. Nothing was too impossible. And if Xia Chengling was still alive, could Master Dao Fei be? She shuddered. If they've managed to live on all these years and amassed this much power, the future was even more terrifying than she had initially thought.

"What does the elder Xia look like?"

Gidget quickly typed into what Jinlei had learned was a 'phone' and showed Jinlei a portrait of the patriarch.

Jinlei breathed a sigh of relief. The patriarch didn't look like Xia Chengling's father. Perhaps who she saw wasn't Xia Chengling after all. Or maybe she was a reincarnation of her childhood rival turned evil incarnate. Nevertheless, one thing's for sure—the Xia dynasty had grown so powerful that it had become the most important conglomerate in the world. And what of the Ling clan?

"We at the Xia Corporation are here to serve you. One innovation at a time," Xia Chengling's lookalike and her brother said in tandem before the screen faded into another series of moving pictures.

"We should go," declared Jinlei, eager to find out what became of the Ling clan. She took one last look at Corp. X's soldiers, and a few of them turned to look her way. The uneasy feeling of being watched came back, and she hurried in the opposite direction. She couldn't shake the feeling that something was coming after her as predatory stares continued to bore into her back.

XI

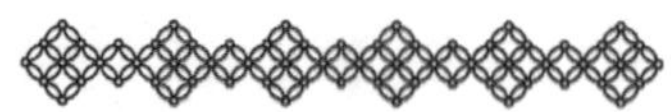

Gidget and Chains led Jinlei to an underground network of speeding receptacles. They tapped their palms on a machine, and somehow, the barriers in front of them opened. For a moment, Jinlei forgot her unsettling nerves. She hung back, distracted by all the machinery and people coming and going. Gidget grabbed her arm and urged her on.

They made their way to a waiting area, when a speeding long, white canister zoomed and stopped in front of them. Apparently, it was the hyper-bullet train they were supposed to take. Jinlei hesitated about getting on.

"Are you sure it's safe?" she asked worriedly.

Gidget gave a little laugh. "Of course! Millions of people ride the subway every day. Come on!"

Jinlei let herself be led inside, where they sat on an empty bench. The inside wasn't as sleek white as the outside, but screens continued to flash advertisements inside the trains. Jinlei was somewhat disappointed that she didn't get to see anything out the window. Only concrete tunnels and the occasional lights passed her by until the train stopped at the next station. She narrowed her eyes at a small sign she noticed overhead: "Powered by Corporation X." She frowned in disbelief. Corp. X really did extend their tentacles everywhere.

As the train sped along and lights whizzed by, it reminded her of her recent travel through a certain other portal. She shut her eyes, trying not to hurl at the memory of being shaken and spun around in her journey through eternity. Thankfully, her headache and nausea had subsided to a mere pulsing annoyance. However, the feeling of being watched came back.

All of a sudden, she felt the train speed up, screeching against the wind. She fell sideways against Chains, who caught her easily. Her eyes flew open in the same instant the train slowed as if coming to a stop. Everyone else seemed to slow down as well. Only she was moving at normal speed, as if she didn't march to the same beat as everyone else. A black and purple cloud of smoke emerged from the man in front of her. Was this man on fire? Jinlei frantically looked around for help or an escape route. If the man was lighting something on fire, everyone in this enclosed space would burn up in flames.

The man got up and lunged at her. With quick reflexes, Jinlei evaded, and the man fell over on the bench. Everyone gasped. Someone screamed. Everybody started to move at the same speed again.

"Are you okay?" she asked, adrenaline pumping in confusion.

The man didn't answer, got up and lunged at her again. Jinlei noticed the man's eyes, which seemed to be clouded over in black and purple smoke as well. It was strange, to be sure. But what was stranger was the relentless way in which he kept coming at her, and only her. The man's moves took on a sophistication, attacking her and hitting her with more precision. The man took off the belt around his pants, and Jinlei realized that he was determined to inflict serious damage on her.

The belt sliced the air and welted Jinlei's arms and legs. Jinlei gave a yelp. This time, she wouldn't hold back as the man obviously fought with skill.

She circled the man's arm with her leg, effectively blocking his whipping arm. She wrapped the belt around his wrist as she elbowed him in the face and followed up with successive blows. The man soon collapsed to the ground, unconscious.

Heavily breathing, Jinlei quickly walked back to Chains and Gidget, wishing to hide from all the stares.

"Watch out!" Chains called out.

Jinlei couldn't react quickly enough as something tightened around her neck. The man's belt. She gasped, trying to stretch out her neck, grasping at the noose around her neck. In seconds, she felt the belt loosen up, and she fell to the floor, choking for air.

Chains restrained a woman who was wrestling against him. She clawed at the air, trying to get at Jinlei. A similar black and purple smoke surrounded her, and her eyes had the same smoky look as the unconscious man beside Jinlei.

The train announced the next stop. Jinlei quickly got to her feet and touched a pressure point on the woman's neck. The woman instantly went limp. She was out cold.

As soon as the train doors opened, all three were out the door. There were uniformed officials waiting on the platform. Some officials boarded the train and others stopped some passengers to talk to them. Some passengers pointed to the three of them.

"Someone must have called the cops. Let's get out of here," Chains urged.

They scrambled to the nearest exit, dodging the stream of people coming and blocking their way. Somewhere behind them, they heard angry shouts. "Hey! You there! Stop! STOP!"

They ran up the stairs, pushing people out of the way.

"STOP!" From the sound of their voices, the officials were close on their heels.

Chains and Jinlei shoved some people onto the officers, making them all stumble down the stairs. That bought the trio some time.

"Stop them!" someone shouted. But no one dared to. From the sound of it, Jinlei figured they were well ahead of the officials.

Chains led the way, curving a corner and emerging onto a different street.

"I think we've lost them," said Gidget as she peered behind them.

They slowed down to catch their breaths.

"What was that about?" asked Chains.

Jinlei frowned. "I don't know." She explained how everything seemed to speed up and then slow down, and the black smoke around the people who attacked her.

Chains scratched his head. "Weird. I didn't see any of that. All I saw was the guy suddenly come at you."

"You didn't see the smoke?"

"Nope," said Chains. Gidget shook her head.

Gidget rearranged her glasses as she thought about what she had just heard. "Looks like only you saw time speed up and then slow down. I wonder, could it have something to do with your time travel?"

"Maybe you've angered the gods of time by being here," Chains said offhandedly, intending to lighten the mood.

Jinlei rubbed her arm, the welt from earlier stinging under her jacket. "Possibly." It sounded improbable, but there might be a ring of truth in it.

Chains blinked. "Oh, you don't actually think . . . ? But that's crazy!"

"I guess we'll just have to wait and see," said Jinlei. "Hopefully,

I can find my mother's spell before anything else happens."

"Let's hope so," Gidget agreed.

XII

They wandered around the city, trying to figure out how to get to Jinlei's old estate. Jinlei found it hard to believe that they made it here in less than an hour when it used to take her almost a week to travel back and forth to the capital.

Water Drop Village had become Water Drop City. It had retained its name but had grown into a vast metropolis. It was almost as crowded and noisy as the capital. There were almost no empty spaces, the landscape devoid of plush greenery such as the way Jinlei remembered. Despite the marvels of the modern world, her heart ached for the things of the past. They may not have had the conveniences and shiny distractions of modern life, but things were simpler back then. Jinlei would trade all the train rides and youth preservation creams for her family and friends back home.

The image of Jun in his sophisticated yet stylish robes flashed through her mind. She never appreciated the graceful elegance with which he carried himself. So different from the unrefined, rough urchins she saw on the streets. Her heart gave an unexpected leap as she remembered the gallant way in which he saved her and her mother just in time. She wondered if they had defeated Dao Fei. She had determined to stop referring to the old priest as Master Dao from now on. He no longer deserved the respect. Between her mother and Jun, Dao Fei wouldn't stand a chance, even with his enhanced demon powers. She hoped it wouldn't be long before she saw them again.

"This is the second biggest city in China," said Gidget. "Corp. X's second biggest research and development operations are here."

"Not a surprise if the Xias are in charge. It figures they wouldn't stray too far from home," Jinlei replied absent-mindedly, still distractedly taking in the unfamiliar scenery with disdain.

"So where is this estate of yours? I'll try to look for it here," Gidget asked as she took out her phone.

"It was east of the River Yi. The Xia estate used to be west of the river."

"Ah! Got it." Gidget grinned. "Follow me."

They walked past concrete buildings, city streets, and road traffic. Jinlei started to recognize her bearings when they reached the middle of the river, where a footbridge led to the other side.

"We're on the west side," said Gidget.

"Yes. I used to stand there across the bridge, and look to the Xia estate over here. There. See? That's where their house used to be." Jinlei pointed to a large complex not far from the bridge where now a towering walled-off, white building stood, similar to the Corp. X headquarters in the capital.

Gidget looked at the phone device in her hands. "Yeah, says here this area is Xiahe District, the richest and biggest district in the city, home to Corp. X's headquarters in Water Drop City, as well as Water Drop University and many high-end department stores, malls and other amenities."

Soldiers clad in black armor similarly patrolled the area around the building. Some of them strutted around the river, making street peddlers move and demanding payment for illegal operations.

Two young girls were on a bench, whispering and pointing at the soldiers. One girl said, "There they go again. Harassing honest people who just want to make a living. I mean, they're private security, not city cops. They have no right to demand payment. It's a shame no one's powerful enough to stand up to them."

"One did. Yesterday," the other girl responded with a hint of delicious gossip in her voice. "I saw it with my own eyes. This mysterious stranger came to the rescue, looking like a real-life prince."

The other girl replied just as enthusiastically. "I heard the soldiers were harassing some girls, and some guy fought them off with nothing but his fists. And won!"

"He sure did. Even with the soldiers' shields and weapons, this guy ran circles around them. I guess there's still a few decent guys in the world," the girl sighed. "Why can't there be more guys like him?"

Chains's ears perked up upon hearing the girls' conversation, and he grinned. "Well, girls, you don't need to look very far . . . hey!"

Jinlei pulled him back before he could make a fool of himself. "You're welcome."

"I didn't thank you," said Chains. He took one last look at the girls, his eyes glistening like a puppy.

"You should thank me for saving you from a few slaps in the face," Jinlei retorted.

Chains blinked dumbfoundedly. Then a smile spread across his face. "Oh, I see what's happening. Don't worry your pretty little head over me. I have plenty of love to give!" He spread his arms wide as if to engulf Jinlei in a big hug.

Jinlei put a hand to his face to stop him. Evidently, he had forgotten how strong she was, as he found his face squashed against her palm like doughy bread. "Let's go," she sighed, walking across the bridge.

Gidget looked at her phone again. "I guess we're going to Lao Cheng district, the poorest district in the city . . ." she abruptly stopped herself when she saw Jinlei stiffened.

As they reached the other side, a market square greeted them. Jinlei hated to admit it, but she could see why this would be considered the poorest district in the city. The old village market where Jinlei had spied on Xia Chengling was now filled with gaudy signs, cheap décor and careless litter. The glaring shininess of this district with its cheap lights highlighted its garishness, while the shininess of the Xiahe District highlighted its stylish, glossy modernity.

Jinlei picked up her pace, dying to know whatever became of her old home in the future.

When they finally reached the place where her home was supposed to be, Jinlei's footsteps slowed to a disappointed stop.

"It's not here," she declared softly, her shoulders slumping in dismay. She supposed it would be too much to expect for her home to remain the way it was, even as modernity rose up everywhere else. In its place was a nondescript concrete building that showed cracks on its weathered walls.

Before anyone could stop her, Jinlei rapped on the door, curious to see who'd be inside. A bent, old woman opened the door halfway. "What do you want?" she demanded.

"Excuse me," Jinlei began. "Do you know the people who used to live here? The Ling clan, once the most prominent house in Water Drop Village . . ."

The door shut in her face before she was finished.

"That was rude," she huffed.

"Come on." Gidget took her elbow. "It looks like government housing that's been around for ages. No one would know what happened to the Ling house. But the good news is I have enough to go on." She gave Jinlei a mysterious smile. "Let's take a break there."

They made their way back to the busy market square. Stalls of various bootleg goods lined the streets, along with humble eateries, teahouses, and entertainment centers with flashing neon lights.

Gidget picked a run-down café that had seen better days. Bright, colorful lights masked its bleak exterior of weathered walls and chipping paint. Smoking delinquents loitered outside its doors and littered the streets. Inside was dark as night, despite its flashy exterior. The only lights that shone were from screens on the tables and the neon lights behind the counter.

"Café or games?" the proprietor asked as the trio came up to the counter.

"Café. I got my own computer," said Gidget.

The proprietor nodded as he yawned. "Sit anywhere you like. Your waitress will take your order."

They picked a table on the far corner by the window, where a sliver of light came through for Gidget to work. She explained to Jinlei that they were in an internet gaming café and bar, where people could socialize while they played games and drank. One end of the café consisted of tables filled with computers and comfortable, ergonomic chairs, while the other end only had tables and chairs like a normal restaurant. People had the option to go back and forth between the gaming area or the restaurant/café, or they could also order food and drinks while they played video games.

Jinlei still didn't quite understand Gidget's modern jargon but smiled and nodded as if she did. She didn't think she would stay in this world for much longer and, therefore, didn't feel the need to familiarize herself too much with the newfangled technology and the way people spoke, which she found to be rather vulgar.

A waitress came to their table and took their order. Gidget took out her computer while Chains and Jinlei scarfed down the food as soon as it came. Jinlei hadn't realized how hungry she was. She hadn't eaten much because of her nausea, but now that it was all but gone, she found herself regaining her appetite.

"For a noble, you eat just like the rest of us," Chains remarked as he licked the meat off its bones.

Jinlei slurped the last droplets of her extra-large spicy beef noodle soup. "Technically, I hadn't eaten for a thousand years. What is that?" she asked curiously.

"Fried chicken. Here, try it." He pushed the basket of fried chicken across to Jinlei.

She picked up a leg, sniffed it, and decided it didn't smell bad at all. She inhaled the intoxicating mix of spices and fried skin that made her mouth water. She bit into the chicken's crispy skin seasoned with five spice, and her senses opened up, as if she had traveled to a whole new world all over again.

Chains grinned. "Good, eh?"

Jinlei nodded enthusiastically and took another piece after she finished off the first one. Gidget, who sat by the window beside her, was busy clacking away on her computer, taking a few bites of her sandwich as she worked.

"Gidget here is one hell of a hacker. She'll find you what you need in no time," Chains said in between bites.

Hacker? It was another one of those words Jinlei didn't know. Chains tried explaining it to her, but it seemed to her that he knew about as much as she did. Nevertheless, the important thing was Gidget knew what she was doing, and somehow the little gadget she was clacking into (which Jinlei learned was called 'typing') contained all the world's knowledge, though it apparently took a certain kind of genius to manipulate it and extract the precious information it contained. Jinlei still found it hard to believe how you could get anything in the modern world with just the touch of your fingertips. Looking at the gaming café side of the room, everyone looked like drones, mindlessly pushing buttons and typing into their keyboards as they spoke to people on the things around their heads, called 'earphones' or 'headsets.'

Jinlei shook her head in morbid wonder. "But why don't you just talk to your friends face-to-face instead of talking to them through your 'headphones?'"

Chains sighed as he tried explaining again. "Like I said, you can't really take your eyes off the screen when you're gaming, so you have to talk through the headsets."

"But I don't understand how playing war through a screen could be fun? Jun and I would practice our martial arts moves on each other, and we actually fought opponents in real life. We'd actually *feel* the sensation of being hit and giving the same in return—of bones cracking, flesh tearing, maybe taste a little blood. Now, *that's* fun!"

Chains chuckled. "You're one violent chick. I don't blame you. But you know, not everyone could be as powerful as you."

"Why not?" she continued to argue. "Everyone could be, with the right training and discipline. That's what being a martial artist is all about—to be able to achieve your highest self through self-cultivation."

"Yeah, well. Most people don't have the time or the discipline. Most people are busy running the rat race—getting through school on top of part-time jobs, or people with full-time jobs who need a second job just to make ends meet and provide for their families."

"But you've done it. With the way you fight, I know you've undergone some hard training." Jinlei finished the last of her chicken and wiped her hands clean.

"Not really. I didn't go through the sort of training you're thinking of. I didn't have martial arts teachers or sparring partners. The streets taught me." He had a pensive, faraway look in his eyes. He was normally a happy-go-lucky guy who didn't seem to have a care in the world, and this unexpected side surprised Jinlei. "Me and Gidget—we don't have school or a regular job. We're what you'd call stray dogs. The forgotten."

Jinlei's eyes softened. She realized she hadn't really appreciated her lot in life, nor could she really understand how Gidget and Chains lived and survived on the streets. Despite the conveniences of the modern world, she probably lived a more comfortable life than they did, with everything handed to her and attendants who waited on her hand and foot.

"I'm sorry," Jinlei said, her eyes downcast with guilt. She must have sounded insensitive to Chains. She realized that his tough exterior was due to him living the hard life and surviving on the streets.

Chains chuckled good-naturedly. "Hey, don't worry about it. Like I said, we get by. Speaking of stray dogs." He nodded to Jinlei's side.

An argument was brewing at a few tables to the right. A customer started raising his voice. "You gotta be kiddin' me! First, you make us wait, now you give us the wrong order? I said I wanted a cheeseburger, not a hamburger. Where's the cheese?"

"I'm sorry, sir," the waitress bowed as she apologized. "I'll take it back and bring you . . ."

"No, no, no! I'm not waiting another hour for your lousy service!"

"I'll tell the kitchen to make it quick . . ."

"You do that. How hard is it to remember to put cheese on a burger? Are you an idiot? No wonder you're just a waitress. I guess you don't have enough brain cells to do anything else."

"I'm sorry . . ." the waitress said again, her voice cracking, clearly on the verge of tears.

"Oh, for . . . Stop crying your stupid face out!" The customer slammed a fist as he went on berating the server.

"I'll get my manager . . ." the server managed to babble out in between sobs.

Before she could turn to leave, the customer grabbed her wrist roughly, preventing her from moving. "No, you deal with me right now."

"Please, sir . . ."

Jinlei was about to get up and do something even ruder to the customer when a slice of bread came flying in the air, aiming straight for the customer's face. It connected with a loud 'thump.'

The customer got up angrily, shouting, "Who did that?! Who?!" Another slice of bread came zipping through, straight into the customer's open mouth, effectively silencing him.

Jinlei saw who had launched the bread like a shooting arrow. A mysterious figure seated a few tables away was casually eating what Jinlei deduced was a 'hamburger,' though he was only eating the meat since he had thrown away the buns. He looked calm and indifferent, but Jinlei knew he possessed great martial abilities for him to be able to use something as soft and delicate like bread as a weapon. He was seated far enough that Jinlei couldn't see the details of his face, but he had thick black hair with hints of reddish brown. He wore jeans with a black shirt and a black leather jacket with an attached hood. Even from a distance, she could tell he had an imposing presence, yet he clearly stood for justice when he saved the waitress from further abuse. Could this be the mysterious stranger the girls by the river were talking about?

The angry customer stomped over to the mysterious stranger as the waitress pleaded behind him, "Please, sir, there's no fighting in here . . ."

"You think you're funny? Why don't you face me like a man?" the angry customer demanded, hovering over the mysterious stranger.

The waitress got in between them. She pleaded with the stranger to stop fighting. "Please . . . my manager won't like it. I could lose my job . . ."

"Don't worry, miss," the stranger told her, his voice deeper than Jinlei expected. "I have no intention of fighting anyone weaker than me."

"What did you say?!"

The angry customer made to grab the stranger's hood, but the stranger sidestepped, blocked his arm, and twisted it. The stranger had the angry customer's arm in a lock and pushed him face-down onto the table. However, they had accidentally knocked over the waitress by accident. Good thing Jinlei saw it coming. She was on her feet in an instant and managed to catch the waitress's fall.

"Are you okay?" Jinlei asked as she helped the waitress to her feet.

"Yes, thank you," the waitress said gratefully.

"Aaahhh!" the angry customer protested as the manager finally came over.

"What is the meaning of this?" the manager demanded.

The angry customer spit out a series of angry rants, blaming the waitress for her incompetence, then the stranger for hitting him.

"Alright, alright!" the manager boomed. "You and you," he pointed to the waitress and the stranger. "First, apologize to this gentleman."

Jinlei gaped at him. She rose up to their defense, wanting to explain how the customer had been out of line, but the manager immediately cut her off as if she were some worthless bug. He didn't even have the decency to acknowledge her presence and waved her away dismissively. Jinlei's mouth dropped open in shock. She still couldn't get used to how rudely people treated each other in the modern world.

"I don't think I should be apologizing for something that wasn't my fault," the stranger said coolly. "But don't worry. I'm taking my leave." He paid his bill and handed a generous tip to the waitress. "For your trouble."

"Hey, we're not done here," the angry customer insisted.

"Yes, we are. You and I both know that the only reason you still have your limbs is because I refuse to waste my energy on someone who obviously can't fight back. Now, go back to your table like the little man you are and wait patiently for your order while you still have your pride left." The stranger stared impassively at the angry customer. He had the sort of look that could stop anyone in their tracks, and not just because of his deep, enigmatic eyes. His presence alone was intimidating. Even Jinlei wanted to shrink in his presence, and she wasn't easily intimidated.

The angry customer himself knew that he was outclassed. It was merely out of pride that he complained to the manager in a loud voice. The weakest dogs really barked more than they bit.

Even the manager hesitated to argue with the stranger. To save face and to make it seem like he had handled the situation instead of the mysterious stranger who was making it out the door, the manager said, "Well, I hope the problem has been resolved, sir. Please be seated. Your dinner will be on the house."

"Thank you," the angry customer replied gruffly. He also went along with the masquerade, pretending that the manager had sorted out his problem and that he hadn't just been publicly humiliated, being called out for oppressing those weaker than him when he was obviously a weak person himself.

Jinlei was glad she hadn't had to deal with the mysterious stranger herself, though she felt a pull as he walked out the door without looking back. Without even a second glance at her. Master Fu always taught her that martial arts was not about showing off one's skills and that one should never fight unless one had to. But she had never wanted so badly to square off with someone. She felt that she could show him a thing or two.

She shook her head as she flopped back down at their table. "I'll never understand why people like that insist on bullying others when they can't handle the same thing being done to them."

Chains shrugged, casually drinking his water. "In this world, you take what little power you can get."

Jinlei sighed at Chains's indifference. She guessed he was used to explosive displays like the one they just witnessed. On the other hand, Gidget was still hard at work at her computer, as if she hadn't seen or heard anything at all.

Chains noticed Jinlei wondering about Gidget. "When she gets in the zone, she doesn't notice anything. That's why she needs me around, to let her know when the zombies start attacking," he joked.

"It's amazing." Jinlei nodded. "Say, how did you two meet?"

"In an orphanage," Chains replied.

Jinlei brought down her glass. Her ears perked up with interest. "Really?"

"Yeah." Chains absent-mindedly nibbled on a bone. "We were

just kids then when we happened to arrive around the same time. She was friends with my sister . . ." He coughed suddenly as he caught himself.

Jinlei raised her eyebrows. "Where's your sister now?"

"Somewhere. Hey, any luck there, G?" Chains quickly changed the subject.

It was apparent that Chains didn't wish to talk about his sister, but Jinlei wondered why. She supposed he would tell her in time.

"Yes. I got good news and bad news. The bad news is there's no living records of the Ling or Hu clans. Apparently, nothing survived during that attack at your home. The whole compound was burned down and everything in it. It's safe to say that none of your mother's records probably survived," said Gidget, stretching after being slumped over the computer for a while.

"But how can you know that for sure?" Jinlei asked, still not understanding how Gidget could have found that out from a few clicks on a keyboard.

"Here." Gidget turned the laptop so Jinlei could see. "I hacked into the local university's research archives. See? I located the site of your house and they have a simulation of how the site looked like over the years." She played the simulation for Jinlei.

Jinlei's eyes widened as she saw the site undergo changes from the present day all the way back to the past. It went from the dilapidated building it was today, to its fresh construction, to a brick building with a traditional curved roof, to an empty lot. Her face moved closer to the screen as the date flashed: 750 AD, the thirty-eighth year of Emperor Xuanzong's rule. It showed the site covered in black ash. She found it difficult to decipher the modern Chinese characters, but she somewhat got the main idea. A paragraph on the side briefly explained that what was once the sprawling estate of a noble was burned by local rebels in an uprising. It went on to say that the noble's family and anyone connected to him had been executed for his corruption and betrayal against the empire. After the noble's execution, Count Xia Sheng and his army of empire loyalists stamped out the rebellion and peace was restored to the county. There was no record of the noble family's name, as it was lost during the chaos of that brief conflict. The emperor recognized Count Xia Sheng's contributions, named him a marquis, and granted him some territory. Since then, the gods had continued to look favorably upon the Xia family, whose contributions to the country continue to be felt to this day.

Jinlei's mouth dropped open in disbelief, her fingers gripping the sides of the table in low, seething anger. She felt personally scandalized at the lies told about her family. There was no mention of Dao Fei, the demon Tao-tie, or the jiangshi during that supposed uprising. Instead, it painted the Xias in a heroic light and her family as lowly traitors.

"This isn't right," she said, her voice shaking. "That isn't what happened at all!"

"What's the good news?" asked Chains, hoping to calm Jinlei down.

Gidget turned the offending computer away from Jinlei. "Well, you say that your mom's magic was only passed down through her line, right? What if we can find surviving descendants of your mom's line?"

Still visibly shaken and with her mind going in different directions, Jinlei barely heard what Gidget said. "But how?"

"DNA testing," Gidget replied simply. "We'd just need to get a kit. I'm sure we can find one around here. We can take a swab of your DNA. Once we get the results, we can isolate the genes from your mom's side and cross-reference it to the government's database or any other databases out there to see if we can find a match."

Jinlei was already reeling from the injustice her family had suffered, and Gidget's modern speak only added to her confusion. All this tension made her want to break something, fight something or shake some sense into the silly inhabitants of this world. But that wasn't fair to Gidget, who was only trying to help her. She forced herself to relax her hands and the tension in her arched back, which was ready to pounce at any moment.

"It's worth a shot," Chains nodded encouragingly.

"Did your mom have any relatives? Any others who might have known about the magic?" Gidget asked.

"Yes, the Hu clan had a wide reach, though not everyone would have been taught such obscure magic. But I'm sure someone else other than my mother would have known about it."

Jinlei took a deep breath. She felt like a rabbit being led by a tiger, but she had to trust them to navigate this strange world. Besides, they seemed to know what they were talking about and both of them seemed to think that whatever they just said was a good idea. She hoped it really was.

XIII

The trio walked around the market square, looking for portable DNA testing kits. The market was haphazardly organized into different sections—clothes, jewelry, electronics, etc. The electronics and technology side had stalls and stalls of computers, phones, stereos and all types of gadgets.

After they found what they were looking for, they found a cheap room for the night. There was a budget hostel just a few blocks from the market square. Gidget paid ¥300 a night for the three of them to share one room.

The room was a little better than the room they had in the capital. There was at least a bed instead of just a mattress on the floor. It took up half of the room. One thing Jinlei did like about the modern world was the soft mattresses. She hadn't realized what she had been missing—it was like sleeping on a cloud. Back home, they only had wooden beds.

There was a table across the bed for Gidget to set up her laptop, as well as a closet beside the table to store their things. Still, it was dark with fluorescent lights that flickered on and off, and dingy with a faint odor of old mold. The door to the bathroom was right next to the main door. Jinlei opened the bathroom door and the lingering stench of dried urine made her nose crinkle. Gidget showed her how to turn on the faucet and the shower. She spent some time turning the water on and off, fascinated as the water flowed easily by her command. She had never been so excited to take a bath in her life.

After they dropped their bags and settled into their room, Gidget instructed Jinlei, "Here, open wide."

Confused, Jinlei did what she was told. Gidget swiped a stick around her mouth. Gidget called it a 'cotton swab.'

The DNA testing kit contained a portable sequencing device, which Gidget plugged into her phone. She secured the DNA sample into the sequencing device. "Now, we just have to wait. It should be ready in a few hours."

Chains stretched out on the floor. The bed was only big enough for two. "Good. Man, I'm beat."

"Right. We should get some rest. It'll be another long day tomorrow," Gidget agreed.

Jinlei and Gidget took the bed while Chains lay on the floor. The hostel gave him extra comforters and pillows to sleep on.

* * *

The next day, the DNA results were waiting for them by the time they woke up. Around lunchtime, they headed to the same gaming café as yesterday for Gidget to conduct her research.

"This will take a while. Why don't you guys go around for a bit while I finish up here?" Gidget said after they had eaten a hearty lunch.

That suited Jinlei just fine. Even as a noble back home, she was an active girl who'd much rather play outside than embroider inside. As they walked the modern streets of her hometown, she was still amazed at how bright and noisy everything was. Yet, all the noise carried with it desperate undertones of despair. Who knew that this was how the future looked like?

"Hey, come here. I'll show you something." Chains led her to another indoor entertainment center.

Jinlei frowned. She was certain there was absolutely nothing in here that could interest her.

"This is what gaming is." He flashed a toothy grin.

He led her to a large gaming machine and explained to her the rules. It was a fighting game, and Jinlei chose a female game character dressed in modern Manchu clothing, her hair tied up in two buns on the sides of her head.

She was reluctant at first, but Jinlei's competitive nature quickly took over as she kept challenging Chains to another fight. She wasn't satisfied until she won two rounds in a row.

"Told you you'd like it." Chains grinned smugly.

"Still doesn't substitute for the real thing," Jinlei said, not wanting to admit how much fun she actually had.

Next, Chains led her to a machine with balls and a ring at the other end. "You shoot these basketballs into the hoop. The player who gets the most balls in wins. Simple."

Jinlei cracked her knuckles. Simple indeed. But she soon found it wasn't all that easy after all. The balls easily bounced off the rings, and she had to shoot as many as she could before the timer buzzed.

"HAHAHAHA!" Chains guffawed out loud, gloating.

"One more," Jinlei said through gritted teeth.

Chains himself was mercilessly competitive, clearly enjoying having the upper hand. For all her supposed love of competition, Jinlei was a sore loser. Why couldn't Chains just go easy on her for once? He knew she was just a beginner, and he'd had years of practice over her. Still, he continued to taunt her by shooting the balls one-handed while not even looking at the ring!

Jinlei recalled how Jun used to let her win sometimes. Such was his gentle and endearing nature, always considerate of others. Every bit the gentleman. The complete opposite of this buffoon. Jinlei finally got tired of losing and walked away grumpily.

"Hey, wait up!" Chains called after her.

Jinlei continued walking in a huff.

"Come on, it's just a game." Chains nudged her good-naturedly but still with the proud smile of a rascal.

Jinlei continued to sulk. "I bet I could win against you in a real fight."

Chains chuckled, amused. "Sure. But you may want to hold off on pummeling me until after we find what you're looking for."

"Fine. It's a deal." She smiled, finally giving in to Chains's easygoing character.

They walked around a bit more, Jinlei taking in the grimy streets with the cramped buildings, flashing bright neon lights and noisy people. They walked by the river, which wasn't the clear blue she remembered, but a cloudy green, she noticed with dismay. Jinlei pointed out places and things to Chains, describing to him how they used to be. "There used to be a pagoda over there." She pointed up the river, where now a barbershop resided, marked by a pink barber's pole.

"*Er*, yeah. Let's go this way." Chains steered her the opposite way.

"Over there was the Heaven and Earth Temple . . ." Jinlei stopped herself upon seeing the place where the temple used to be— because it was exactly as it had always looked. "It's still there." She turned to Chains for an explanation.

"Yeah. Looks like it's always been there." Chains shrugged,

unable to explain further.

"But why? When everything else has changed?" Jinlei's heart skipped a beat, not wanting to acknowledge what she had wondered about in the back of her mind. Demons tended to live for a long time. She knew Dao Fei had become powerful because of Tao-tie, but she didn't know the extent of the power he had acquired. It was entirely possible that Tao-tie could have turned Dao Fei into a demon himself. And if so . . . Jinlei shuddered. And if Dao Fei was still alive, what could he be doing in this modern world?

They walked closer to the temple but found they couldn't proceed any further.

"It's closed. It's already after five. I guess the day just flew by," Chains said, reading the sign by the entrance. "But it looks innocent enough."

"I agree." Jinlei didn't sense any malevolent energy around the temple. Perhaps she was being paranoid. There was no way Dao Fei could have survived for thirteen hundred years, could he?

"Let's head back. G must be waiting for us," said Chains.

They made their way back to the gaming café. Gidget happily waved to them when she saw them walk in.

"Good news," Gidget started, the hint of excitement tingling her voice. "I found a match."

They placed an order for a basket of fried chicken and milk teas before Gidget went on with her findings. "I did a little bit of digging. Turns out—your mom's lineage was all but wiped out—" She paused, noticing Jinlei's body tense up. She coughed uncomfortably and quickly continued, "Well, anyway, there's still hope. Since we did the mtDNA Test for specifically tracing your maternal line, I found one person with a strong matching mtDNA sequence to yours that belongs to the same haplogroup."

Jinlei tried not to let her impatience show. It frustrated her whenever anyone started throwing away unfamiliar technological terms.

"Long story short," Gidget continued, noticing Jinlei's growing anxiousness. "Her name is Wang Bai. She runs a traditional Chinese medicine shop just a couple blocks away."

Jinlei let out a relieved breath, finding it almost hard to believe that Gidget really did find a direct descendant from her maternal lineage. It still wasn't guaranteed that her distant relative called Wang Bai would know anything about her mother's magic, but it was worth investigating. She wanted to give Gidget a tight hug but restrained herself according to propriety, though she had a sneaking suspicion that the modern world didn't observe such propriety. Maybe in time, she could someday give a friend a hug. Who knows? Regardless, the weight on her heavy heart was somewhat alleviated. Even if Wang Bai didn't have the magic, this new information gave Jinlei a surge of hope that she would be able to find a way to get back home. She was grateful that she wasn't so alone in this strange place.

Gidget smiled at Jinlei and gave her hand a squeeze. Jinlei squeezed back. A hand squeeze was a good start.

With great hope for the future, all three dug into their delicious, crispy fried chicken and ate and drank merrily.

Now that she felt lighter, Jinlei noticed something she hadn't noticed earlier. The mysterious stranger was back. He was sitting a few tables to the right of them. He had his hood up, but that outfit and that presence was unmistakable. Her heart gave an unexpected leap as she hadn't expected to see him again.

"Hey? Earth to Jinlei," Chains waved a hand in front of her.

Jinlei realized that Chains had asked her a question, but she hadn't heard it.

"What are you looking at? Oh, is that the same guy from yesterday?" Chains asked, much too loudly, in Jinlei's opinion.

The stranger seemed to hear Chains as his hood tilted slightly to the side. She gave Chains a look to keep his voice down.

"Why are you staring?" Chains whispered loudly, which wasn't any better than the regular volume of his voice.

Gidget gave Jinlei a smile that seemed to suggest she knew something Jinlei didn't. Jinlei didn't like that look and scowled at her.

In a low voice, Jinlei replied, "I'm staring because he's staring at that guy for some reason."

Chains and Gidget both turned to look and not subtly at all.

Even though the stranger had his hood on, Jinlei could tell that he was alert and seemed to be watching a gentleman on the other end of the room. The gentleman was dressed in a casual polo shirt and jeans. He had a cap on, so you couldn't see his face. He looked just like any other guy off the streets. There was no reason why anybody would find him of great interest. Before long, a glamorous young lady joined his table. They ate and laughed for a while until it was time to leave.

Jinlei noticed the mysterious stranger get up to follow the couple outside. She didn't have a good feeling about the whole scenario, especially as she knew the mysterious stranger could fight well, and she wasn't sure if the couple could. Acting on pure instinct, Jinlei got up to follow all three out the door.

"Hey, where are you going?" Chains called out from behind her, but she ignored him.

Jinlei looked up and down the street, to her left and right. She saw the outline of a hooded figure disappear around the corner. She hurried to catch up to them.

As soon as Jinlei turned the corner into a hidden alleyway, a scream erupted from the girl. The stranger had the man in a headlock. One twist, and the guy would be dead. In a flash, Jinlei reached for the bladed fans tucked into her pants and threw them at the stranger's arms to loosen his grip, but it was more a distraction than anything. She scaled the wall to reach the stranger in no time and delivered a side kick to his head. The stranger inadvertently let the man go.

"Go! Quickly!" Jinlei urged the couple to leave. The couple held onto each other as they made a run for it.

The stranger was about to chase them down, but Jinlei pulled him back. He tried to shove her arms off him, but she countered with her signature crane strikes. She drew her fingers together, imitating a crane beak, and darted at delicate points at his eyes, behind his ears and neck. He kept her at bay, aggressively striking at her with extended jabs and circular kicks. She noticed the style as the Long Fist style, a long-range fighting system. The Flying White Crane style was great for close ranges, and the Long Fist was a perfect counter to her.

Jinlei swooped with her arms as a crane swoops onto its prey. She feinted successive strikes to the stranger's head and face until she kneed his lower abdomen. She followed through with a leopard paw fist to the same area. The stranger went down but didn't stay there. He whirled on the ground like a windmill, kicking with his legs as the crane swooped from above. Jinlei was caught in the windmill and fell face down. The impact rattled her more than she expected. She stayed down a bit longer than she should have. A leg dove down on her. She rolled over just in time and scrambled to her feet.

The stranger scaled the wall to gain momentum for his extended spinning kick. Jinlei managed to block the kick with her arms but still fell backward from the impact. That gave the stranger just enough time to leap over her on the ground just as Chains showed up. The stranger shoved Chains out of the way as he made his way out of the alley.

Chains wanted to make sure Jinlei was alright, but she got on her feet, trying to catch up to the stranger. When they got out of the alley and scanned the streets, there was no sign of him.

* * *

Back in their rented room, Chains was on his makeshift bed and cracked his neck in a stretch. "What was that back there anyway?"

They all had already changed into their nightclothes. Jinlei and Gidget sat on the bed.

"Yeah. I thought you were chasing after that handsome stranger for other reasons," Gidget said jokingly.

Jinlei didn't appreciate the joke and asked pointedly, "And for what other reason could there be?"

"Nothing, nothing," Gidget waved her hand lightly.

"I told you, I simply don't understand it. After yesterday's incident with that customer and the waitress, I thought he was a good fellow. Next thing you know, he's trying to kill another fellow. Who is this fellow?"

"There are too many fellows in this world," Gidget lamented as she yawned, sprawling out on their bed.

"Are you sleeping?" Jinlei asked, wanting to discuss the situation further.

"Yes, and you should too," Gidget answered, her eyes already closed.

"She's right. We've got another big day tomorrow. Meeting your great great great great niece, right? Is that enough greats?" Chains counted with his fingers from his spot on the floor.

Jinlei sighed as she flopped down on the bed. She supposed

they were right. There was no sense in beating a dead horse, as they say. The important thing was she managed to save the gentleman from getting killed. There was no use thinking about the stranger's motivations. She wasn't the police. And it's not like she would ever see him again.

XIV

After a big brunch, the trio set out to Wang Bai's traditional Chinese medicine shop. It was a few blocks from the market square, on a less busy street.

Door chimes sounded as they opened the door, signaling incoming customers.

Wang Bai was probably in her seventies and walked with a cane. Her hair was dyed black but showed silver streaks. From the self-assured way she carried herself, Jinlei guessed that Wang Bai's vitality defied her age. The medicines in Wang Bai's shop must do wonders for her health, or she must have other hidden abilities. But it was too early to tell. Jinlei found it mind-boggling that she was at the same time older and younger than her kin.

"Discount bins that way," Wang Bai said without a second look at them.

Jinlei gathered her courage and approached the counter. Up close, she could somewhat see the family resemblance. Wang Bai possessed the Hu family's distinctive full cheeks combined with high cheekbones—an apparent contradiction. A water and metal face. Yet, these characteristics exemplified the Hu clan's strengths and weaknesses—the tough metal energy combined with the fluidity of the water energy. Metal represented their determined, active, impatient and domineering energy, while water gave them softness, emotionality, depressive tendencies and their psychic gifts. "Miss Wang Bai . . ." Jinlei began.

Wang Bai was behind the counter, arranging inventory on a shelf when she turned her attention at Jinlei. Her eyes narrowed in suspicion.

Jinlei spoke quickly out of nervousness and to ease Wang Bai's discomfort. "This may sound strange, but I come from the lineage Hu, as in lǎo hǔ for tiger. We're looking for—"

"I'm too busy to play games," Wang Bai abruptly cut Jinlei off and finished arranging the inventory.

"I'm not playing games," Jinlei followed Wang Bai around as the old proprietor emerged from behind the counter and approached another customer, signaling to Jinlei that their conversation was over. "Please, ma'am. I just wanted to ask if you have records of the Hu family's—er—special martial arts knowledge."

"I don't know what nonsense you're talking about," Wang Bai dismissed her impatiently. She avoided Jinlei as she tried to distract herself with various tasks around the shop.

"Are you sure?" Jinlei appealed to Wang Bai desperately, following the old woman around like a lost puppy. "Please, you don't understand. It's very important. There are certain scrolls—secret scrolls—"

Wang Bai cut Jinlei off again. "What's important, young miss, is my place of business. And right now, you're disturbing it. So either you buy something or you leave," she said firmly, rapping her cane on the ground with finality.

"But—"

Wang Bai didn't even give Jinlei a chance to finish her sentence when Wang Bai turned her back on Jinlei. Jinlei's shoulders sank.

Just as Jinlei was about to give up hope on having a productive conversation with Wang Bai, the customer with whom Wang Bai had been speaking turned to Jinlei and tried to grapple her out of the blue. Jinlei's quick reflexes deflected the old lady's arms, but the old lady came back with a vengeance. It was then that Jinlei noticed the black-purple aura surrounding the old lady, just like the other day on the train. Jinlei knew that the old lady must be possessed by something, and Jinlei didn't want to hurt her. The best course of action would be to touch a pressure point. However, whatever possessed the old lady appeared to grant her increased speed and power, making it difficult for Jinlei to maneuver fast enough to touch a pressure point.

Chains came to help, grabbing the old lady from behind. But the old lady reacted quickly and flipped him over. That gave Jinlei enough time to move behind the old lady and touch a pressure point on her spine, effectively freezing her whole body. Jinlei touched another pressure point on her temple to put her to sleep. Jinlei caught the old lady before she hit the ground and sat her in a corner of the shop.

When all that was over, Jinlei guiltily surveyed the broken bins and herbal remedies strewn all over the floor. She apologized profusely to Wang Bai and offered to help clean up.

Wang Bai went to the shop door and turned the 'Open' sign to 'Closed.' She gave Jinlei a stern look and merely said, "Come with me."

Jinlei looked uneasily at Chains and Gidget, who both shrugged. What kind of punishment must Wang Bai have for them? Whatever it was, and if it was anything dangerous, they all shared a look of understanding that they could fight through it. They all decided to follow Wang Bai's lead when she disappeared to the back of the store into a small room. It was a simple office with account books on a table and a shelf against the wall. Wang Bai pulled a book from the shelf, and to their surprise, the shelf opened, revealing a hidden passageway beneath it.

Their eyes widened, wondering if they should continue to follow the inscrutable old lady down a precarious hidden passageway.

"I haven't got all day, you know," Wang Bai remarked impatiently. Upon seeing their hesitation, she pointed out, "You asked about the Hu family's secrets, didn't you?"

Without further hesitation, Jinlei followed her down the stairs in the dark passageway as the bookshelf closed shut behind them. Lights automatically flickered on and off as they made their way down the stairs and the short hallway leading to another room.

"Woah . . ." Gidget remarked impressively.

The room was lit in neon lights, decked out with the latest computers and surveillance technology. The room was rectangular shaped, with the door facing the longest side of the wall. The upper half of the long wall was outfitted with one large long screen. The large screen was divided into dozens and dozens of smaller screens within, each screen showing different sceneries and angles of streets and people. In front of the long screen were four other large computer monitors that took up most of the wall's width, with each monitor having its own keyboard and mouse. Bookshelves also lined the walls, filled with old books and ancient scrolls.

Jinlei could barely contain her joy. They had come to the right place! Soon, she'd make it home. The prospect of saving her family from the monster that was Dao Fei made her lightheaded.

"So this is—records of the Hu family's secrets?" Jinlei breathed, still finding it hard to believe that her family's legacy managed to survive.

"Some of it," Wang Bai confessed. "A lot has been lost over the years—most of them during the Water Drop Rebellion."

Jinlei frowned. "You mean the time Dao Fei attacked us?"

"Same one," Wang Bai agreed. She gestured toward the bookshelves on the wall. "These are the hard copies of the Hu family's martial and mystical arts—journals, instruction manuals and the like." She pointed toward the computers. "They're all backed up on the hard drives."

"So, do you know the Hu family's time travel magic?" Jinlei asked, barely containing the surge of hope she felt in her bones.

Wang Bai gave her a sorry look. "Unfortunately, that was one of the spells that was lost. It was the Hu family's very special secret. It was too precious and too dangerous to be written down. It was only passed down orally and to a select few. After the attack on the Ling family estate, Dao Fei and his allies hunted down the rest of the Hu clan. It was unclear how many survived, but at least one of them did—and that person was my ancestor and the Lady Ling's only sister."

"Auntie Ying!" Jinlei gasped.

Wang Bai smiled. "She saved as many records as she could and wrote down from memory as many things as she could remember. She started this collection off, and her descendants tried to piece together what they could. These records have been passed down in secret from generation to generation until it was passed to me."

"You're amazing," Jinlei said, truly meaning it, tears forming in the corners of her eyes. Her chest swelled with ancestral pride at her family's dedication to keeping their legacy alive. "Do you mind if we go through your books? There must be clues to my mother's magic somewhere in there."

"Sadly, no," Wang Bai said. "Don't waste your time poring over the books looking for clues. I've read every single line countless times over the years—there's none. However, there might be a way to find out."

Jinlei's ears perked up. "How?"

Wang Bai gave her an enigmatic smile. "I'll tell you. But first—you must do something for me."

Jinlei's breath caught in her throat. She should have known it would be too good to be true. A bout of sneaking suspicion crawled up her back. Could this woman really be trusted? "What is it?"

"It's simple, really," Wang Bai said nonchalantly. "There's a certain auction happening a week from today. But it's not just any auction. It's a highly unusual one. Not to mention illegal and highly immoral. The man who runs it is the lowest of the lowlifes. He must be stopped. Help me take him down along with his operations. If you fulfill this task, I'll point you toward the first step in finding your mother's lost magic."

"Oh, come on, lady," Chains protested. "Why make her go through all these hoops? You're family, aren't you?"

"Yes, but I need your help. I can't do it on my own. I'm only an old woman, after all," Wang Bai said without any hint of shame or humility. She stated it as a matter of fact, like reading a newspaper.

Without hesitation, Jinlei agreed, "I accept. If I do as you say and take this man down, you'll tell me how to find my mother's magic?"

Wang Bai smiled though her eyes didn't. "You have my word."

* * *

Over the next few days, they've been going back to Wang Bai's shop to help her clean up and repair the damages. Wang Bai asked Jinlei why the customer attacked her that day. Jinlei explained to her their theories about the black-purple aura and angering the gods of time. Wang Bai kept silent and stone-faced as she listened, and Jinlei couldn't tell if she believed her or not.

Afterward, Wang Bai kept them up to date on the details of the auction. It was highly secret and the time and location wouldn't be disclosed until the last minute. They figured Wang Bai was getting her intelligence by hacking surveillance cameras around the city as well as an insider's phone.

Back in their rented room, Chains wondered out loud, "Why do you think she's so hung up on this auction anyway? And why doesn't she just do it herself?"

"Because *I* have to do it," Jinlei reiterated for the hundredth time. At this point, she didn't much care about the reason behind Wang Bai's methods. She just wanted to get this task over with and find the first clue to her mother's magic.

"Still seems suspicious to me," Chains quipped. "Besides, she's barely told us anything about the auction. We need to know more if we're going to take this guy down."

"Speaking of which, is our equipment ready, Gidget?" Jinlei asked. Unlike Chains, she had no desire to ponder about the old woman's motives.

"All set." Gidget gave a thumbs up. On the big day, Gidget would be doing surveillance together with Wang Bai in an unmarked van close to the auction site, while Jinlei and Chains would be hooked up with hidden cameras and microphones. "We'll be your extra eyes and ears. If anything looks suspicious or anything risky goes down, we'll warn you in advance. Or at least I will. So don't worry."

"I'm not. Especially with you as our extra eyes and ears," Jinlei smiled warmly at Gidget. The more she got to know her brainy friend, the more she adored her. She never had a sister, but if she did, she'd like her to be as smart, capable and endearing as Gidget.

Gidget smiled back at Jinlei, then turned to Chains. "I asked Old Wang Bai the same thing—about why this auction was so important. All she said was if it was allowed to continue, it would be the beginning of the end for humanity." They had started referring to Wang Bai with the honorific, 'Old Wang' or '*Lao Wang*.'

Chains made a face. "Pretty dramatic, don't you think?"

Jinlei was inclined to agree. However, she had a feeling that Old Wang Bai wasn't exaggerating, and that was part of the reason why she deliberately kept them in the dark. But what could be so terrible that she couldn't tell them?

XV

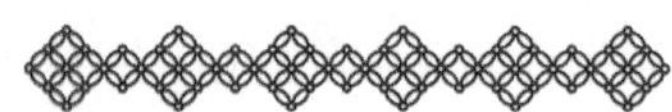

The day before the auction, Wang Bai found out its exact time and location through the catering. They were all gathered at Wang Bai's underground room as she laid out the plan for the next day. Gidget and Wang Bai took seats in front of the large computer monitors, and Jinlei and Chains were seated around them.

"Catering service?" Chains echoed after Wang Bai.

"Yes. These auctions are typically swanky affairs. I checked the high-end caterers and restaurants in the city and found one that had a last-minute request, which they've suspiciously kept off the books. The Jade Palace Garden," Wang Bai explained.

Chains whistled. "That is swanky, alright. It's the most expensive restaurant in the city. Again, what kind of auction is this? I thought you said the guy running it was a lowlife."

"The lowest," Wang Bai concurred. "But this auction is for high-end clients, so don't be surprised when you get there. And please—act with some decency." She made a pointed look toward Chains, who scowled at her.

Wang Bai continued, "The auction is taking place at midnight at the factory district, on the far south end of the River Yi." She turned to her computer and zoomed in on the city map to the exact location of the auction. She pointed on the screen. "There's an abandoned warehouse there, on Peace River Road. You are to show up there as part of the catering crew and get your uniforms for the night."

Gidget clacked on her keyboard and revealed the catering's staff list. She clicked on Chains and Jinlei's photos and said, "We've already tinkered with their staff list and added you two." She turned to Jinlei. "You're Xiao Mei for the night, and Chains, you're Hong Fu."

Wang Bai turned their attention back to her screen. The screen switched from the map to an image of a floor plan. "I managed to get my hands on the warehouse's original floor plans." She pointed to the layout of the second floor. "There are two rooms upstairs. I suspect the auction owner will use one of them as his office for the night. You'll most likely find him there."

Jinlei stared at the screen, memorizing the floor plan. "Great. We should be in and out in no time."

Wang Bai pressed a key on the keyboard and a picture of a skinny, middle-aged man appeared. "This is the head and owner of the auction. He goes by the code name: the Chemist, AKA Chem for short."

Jinlei frowned, unimpressed and somewhat disappointed. Chains suppressed a derogatory chuckle. The Chemist's oiled hair and bespectacled face made him look more like a college professor than a supposed lowlife and underworld boss.

Wang Bai glowered at them with a warning. "Don't underestimate him. He's a lot stronger and more powerful than he looks. Plus, he's surrounded by his personal security at all times. You might find that you'll have to use whatever means necessary to defeat him."

Jinlei doubted it but kept Wang Bai's advice in mind.

"Remember, you must destroy their whole organization."

Wang Bai pressed another key, and the screen gave way to another picture of him carrying a heavy metallic briefcase. "The key to his whole operation is in here. It never leaves his sight. Bring the Chemist back here as well as the briefcase."

Jinlei raised an eyebrow. "Bring him back here?"

"Yes."

"Why not just hand him to the authorities?" Jinlei asked.

"I need him back here," Wang Bai said as if it was the most obvious thing in the world.

Jinlei narrowed her eyes at Wang Bai, wondering what she had up her sleeve.

"What's in the briefcase?" Chains asked.

"That," Wang Bai looked at him pointedly, "is something you don't need to concern yourself with."

Jinlei turned to Chains. "Once we're inside the premises, let's go upstairs and deal with the Chemist right away. Let's get it done and over with it."

Chains clucked his tongue in agreement. "Righty-oh!"

"Be careful," Wang Bai repeated her warning with a serious face. "You may find it's not all that easy."

XVI

The next day, they were all at Wang Bai's secret room to go over plans for the night one last time. At 8:30 PM, they all loaded into the van with the surveillance equipment and arrived at their destination at nine o'clock. Jinlei and Chains's call time was at 10:00 PM and they wanted to arrive in plenty of time to scope out the place.

Gidget gave Jinlei and Chains their earpieces and microphones that used nanotechnology and biomimetic design, rendering them undetectable to the security scanners. They were also given contact lenses which were really micro cameras. It took Jinlei a few tries to put the lenses in. She found the concept utterly baffling. She blinked a few times, trying to get used to the foreign object in her eyes. When Gidget showed her the live feed from her contacts on the computer screen, she could only utter an unintelligible sound. The wonders of modern technology never ceased to amaze and horrify her.

Jinlei and Chains waited with Gidget and Wang Bai in the van, parked a block away from the venue. Wang Bai had hacked into the venue parking lot's cameras, and they watched as trucks, vans and cars were making their way in and out. Some workers unloaded big crates from freight trucks. Others streamed in and out of the docking entrance, unloading various event supplies.

Finally, it was time for Jinlei and Chains to pose as catering servers. They made their way to the rear entrance, where others like them were checking in. The security manning the service entrance consulted their names and faces on his tablet as he checked them in. Another security personnel waved a black device around them before letting them in. Jinlei now knew it to be a metal and radiation scanner. Jinlei breathed a sigh of relief when it didn't beep.

"We're in," Jinlei whispered into the nano-microphone, which blended with her plain white shirt.

There was a buzzing noise in Jinlei's ear, and Gidget's voice came in. "Copy."

They made their way to the makeshift kitchen hidden away from the main event with a makeshift wall. Jinlei put on her white caterer's jacket as she carefully observed the hustle and bustle around her. A flash of reddish-black hair caught her eye, and her heart stopped for a second.

It was the mysterious stranger from the other night. He was also wearing a caterer's jacket. What was he doing here? He wasn't following her, was he?

The head server was giving them instructions for the night, and Jinlei barely paid any attention. Her thoughts were preoccupied with the mysterious stranger and the Chemist's office upstairs. She hadn't seen anyone yet who remotely looked like the Chemist.

After the stage was set, the clock struck midnight, and guests started meandering in. Each of the servers was given a tray of appetizers.

"Remember, circulate! Circulate!" the head server instructed.

As soon as they were on the main floor, Jinlei spotted the mysterious stranger with a food tray.

Jinlei followed the direction to which the mysterious stranger was looking, and her stomach started to churn. The mysterious stranger was eyeing a certain well-dressed man who had no idea he was being watched. Jinlei had always followed her instincts, and they haven't let her down so far. She knew in her gut the well-dressed man was in danger.

The man was dressed in a classy modern suit. Though Jinlei wasn't well-versed in modern clothing, she knew quality when she saw it. No doubt, this man was someone of money and importance. There was something familiar about the way he walked, the way he carried himself, as if he was superior to everyone else in the room. A light of recognition flashed in Jinlei's mind. It was the same man the mysterious stranger had tried to kill the other night. But this time, he was with a different woman. Someone more understated and elegant. Someone in the same class as him.

"Hey," a harsh whisper sounded behind her. Jinlei knew it was Chains but didn't bother to acknowledge a reply.

"I thought we were supposed to look for the Chemist? Like, right now?" Chains continued. He followed Jinlei's intense gaze and landed his eyes on the mysterious stranger.

"Oh, for—" Chains groaned. "What's he doing here? Anyway, it doesn't matter. We need to go. Now. Jinlei."

Jinlei felt Chains nudge her. She blinked as if just waking up. Still, she couldn't just leave when an innocent's life could be in danger.

"See that man?" Jinlei nodded toward the well-dressed man. "That was the same man that guy tried to kill the other night."

"What?" Chains said incredulously. "Listen, I don't want to sound like some cold-blooded . . ."

Chains never got to finish what he was going to say as all the lights dimmed, and a single, prominent spotlight lit up the stage. Everyone turned to the stage set out in the front of the room.

"Ladies and gentlemen!" a loud voice boomed over the speakers. The thunderous voice came from a man in an elegant suit but his face was hidden behind an elaborate mask made of glitters and sparkles and feathers. "I am your host for tonight. The moment you've all been waiting for is here. The silent auction will begin shortly. But first—" the host held out his hand with a flourish "—bring out the goods!"

Half a dozen large crates rolled out from behind the curtains. Once all the crates were firmly settled across the stage, its panels fell dramatically, revealing cages that kept the monstrous things inside from lashing out at the audience. People gasped. Some applauded. Everyone murmured in appreciation and clinked their champagne glasses.

Jinlei and Chains were horrified.

Whatever was inside couldn't be described as human or demon. It was an abomination.

The host's booming laughter filled the whole room. "Feast your eyes on our exclusive creations, courtesy of our big boss and the brains behind our operations, who shall, as always, remain anonymous. Thanks to him, we have created a whole new class of species—the semi-devil! Are they human? Are they demon? They're neither but both at the same time. And now, exclusively for you, our VIP clients, we offer you our one-of-a-kind product you'll never see anywhere else! Which one of you lucky shoppers will get to take home one of these?"

The crowd erupted in cheers and applause.

"Starting with experiment number one here." The host rattled the cage on the farthest left of the stage. The creature snarled and tried to claw at him. The host was never harmed as he deftly moved away. Apparently, he had done this many times before. "Ooh, he's a feisty one, isn't he? Indeed, he used to be a police officer who stuck his nose too closely into our business. I guess he learned his lesson. Hahaha!" The crowd joined in the host's laughter.

Jinlei felt sick to her stomach. Chains clenched and unclenched his fists, trying to control himself. The creatures had the anatomy of a human, but their faces were deformed beyond recognition, with horns sticking out of their heads. Some had scales on their skin. Some had skin colors in different hues, like blue or red. Some had tails.

"What kind of monster could do this?" Jinlei whispered.

"There've been reports of disappearances," Chains whispered back. "I guess this is where some of them ended up."

"Jinlei," Chains said seriously. "We have to find the Chemist now. I don't want to sound cold-blooded," he repeated his thought from earlier, "but if the stranger guy plans to kill the suit guy, the suit guy probably deserves it if he's part of this auction."

Jinlei gulped. She didn't want to admit it, but Chains was probably right. What a cruel world this was when the taking of a human life seemed nothing more than betting in a gambling den.

"Yes. Wang Bai was right. This has to stop," she agreed. Jinlei resolved not to become like any of these technological degenerates gambling on a human life—even if she had the unfortunate fate of staying in the future forever.

While everyone else was still distracted and mesmerized by the host on stage, Jinlei and Chains dropped their trays on a table and made their way up the stairs.

As soon as they reached the top of the stairs, they found two unconscious personnel lying on the floor. Jinlei and Chains exchanged a confused look. Had someone been here before them?

The answer came in the form of sounds of struggle in one of

the rooms. Jinlei and Chains rushed toward the sound.

They arrived just in time. A bespectacled man carrying a briefcase was making his exit through the door. Jinlei recognized him right away as the Chemist. She wasted no time in kicking him back inside. The Chemist stumbled all the way to the center of the room but managed to stay on his feet. Jinlei saw right away that he knew how to fight. This wasn't just some intellectual figurehead who gave orders in the shadows. This was a leader feared by his men.

Jinlei shouldn't have been surprised—but there he was in the same room—the mysterious stranger. He was fighting a big man in a suit and sunglasses.

The man in the nice suit from before cowered against the wall and called out to the man in the sunglasses. "Cypher! The briefcase!"

Cypher shoved the mysterious stranger back and went for the Chemist.

Cypher was presumably protecting the man in the expensive suit. As soon as Cypher abandoned his fight with the mysterious stranger, the mysterious stranger took out a kitchen knife and aimed for the throat of the man in the suit.

Forgetting all her revolting sentiment about the well-dressed people below, Jinlei acted on pure instinct to save a person's life— even if that person was a depraved human being who participated in immoral auctions.

Chains dove for the Chemist's briefcase, three men fighting for one thing.

Jinlei skidded toward the mysterious stranger's legs, wrapped her own legs around his to buckle him down. In close quarters, she jabbed her crane fists into small but critical areas to devastating effect. She didn't just deliver a jab. She jabbed and twisted her rock-hard knuckles, screwing in her fists. All the while, she heard a buzzing in her ear, Wang Bai's voice coming through angrily. But she was too caught up in the fight to make out what was said.

It took him a while, but the stranger unwound his legs from hers to unbalance them both, using the momentary pause in the attacks to get himself back on his feet.

"You," the mysterious stranger growled at Jinlei.

Jinlei was ready for his attack, but he unexpectedly ran past her out the door, chasing after the man in the suit.

"...ase...the...brief..." Wang Bai's voice still couldn't come through clearly enough.

Jinlei ran after the stranger, tackling him back. The stranger snapped his legs at Jinlei and used her extended arms and legs against her. He wound both her arms behind her and pinned her legs with his. He was a whole head taller than her, and the weight of his lean muscles easily immobilized her. The mysterious stranger stared deeply into her eyes, his eyes smoldering with passionate hate. He moved his hands up her body and cupped the back of her neck. Jinlei's eyes widened, unable to fathom what he planned to do.

Out of sheer desperation, she screamed, "No!" and butted her head against his nose.

He reacted with a yelp, and Jinlei threw her full weight and power against his until she was free.

"I'll deal with you another time," the stranger said before leaping over the second-floor railing straight down to the main floor. Some onlookers gasped, but not everyone in the crowd noticed while the loud spectacle was still ongoing.

Seconds later, Cypher came out, Chains on his heels.

"You deal with the Chemist," Chains called back to Jinlei.

The Chemist was racing out the door when Jinlei kicked him back in again.

"You fools!" the Chemist snarled. "Do you realize what you've done?"

"Yes. Stopping this vile thing you've done."

The Chemist laughed ironically. "What I've done is nothing compared to what *they* will do now that the formula is in their hands."

Jinlei frowned, at first not understanding. She scanned the room and realized the briefcase was nowhere to be seen. It wasn't with the mysterious stranger or Chains or Cypher when they ran past her. The sinking realization dawned on her. The man in the suit must have taken it while they were all preoccupied. She remembered briefly seeing the briefcase fly out of the Chemist's hands, then lost track of it after that. That must have been what Wang Bai was trying to tell her.

"Chains will get it back," Jinlei declared.

"Unlikely," the Chemist said, his voice dripping poison. "You'll pay for this, little girl."

Without waiting for him to attack, Jinlei flew toward the Chemist, rapidly striking at his vulnerable points. To her surprise, the Chemist perfectly mirrored her attacks with his defense, as if anticipating her every move. On top of that, he knew the perfect counter to every attack. When she attacked with an underhanded piercing fist to his throat, he shouldn't have seen the deceptive move coming from below. He countered with a side block followed by a wrist grab, which left her torso open for a palm strike.

Jinlei stumbled back, the wind briefly taken from her. Just like her, the Chemist was well-trained in using his upper body strength, with the fluid but stable support of the lower body. They were trained in similar fighting styles. Whereas Jinlei specialized in Flying White

Crane, the Chemist was more of a generalist. He used the White Crane style when necessary but added a mix of modern fighting styles, which Jinlei had never encountered before.

The Chemist didn't give Jinlei time to breathe, rushing in with a combination of close combat crane strikes with fancy footwork that confused her. The footwork tripped her up, and she fell. She lengthened her arm to break her fall. She scrambled to her feet, retreating a few steps back.

The Chemist became the flying white crane itself, soaring in the air before dipping down with his strong, talon-like hands to go in for the kill. At the last second, Jinlei fell on her back, lulling the Chemist into her trap. She whirled her legs to take down the crane's wings, twisted him to a subordinate position, and clawed at his throat. She exerted just enough pressure to cut off the air to his lungs until he fainted.

"Chains! I need you. Now!" Jinlei spoke into her microphone, hoping he'd hear her.

"I'm on my way." In a few minutes, Chains came back, panting as if he'd just been in the fight of his life. Jinlei noticed he didn't have the briefcase and cursed under her breath.

Wang Bai's voice crackled into Jinlei's ear again. Without all the fighting and the moving, Wang Bai's voice came in much sharper and clearer. "You must leave now while the remaining guards haven't been alerted yet."

Remaining guards? Jinlei looked to Chains, who grinned at her.

"Took out the ones patrolling the back elevators and the back alley."

Jinlei smiled at Chains, and he looked away, embarrassed.

Chains stripped the Chemist off his fancy suit jacket and replaced it with a caterer's jacket that he swiped on his way back upstairs. They messed up his hair and took off his glasses. Chains and Jinlei each took one arm on the shoulder and walked him out. If anyone notices them, they'd say the Chemist had too much to drink. Hopefully, they won't have to resort to more violent means of convincing anyone.

They passed one or two people on the way back to the van, but no one stopped them to ask questions. Once safely back in the van, Wang Bai handcuffed the Chemist's hands behind his back, taped his mouth, and put a bag over his head as they made their way back to the basement.

*　*　*

Wang Bai removed the bag covering the Chemist's head. The Chemist at first blinked, not knowing where he was. Slowly, he realized he couldn't move as thick ropes bound him to a chair. He tried screaming, but his screams were muffled against the tape covering his mouth. He looked around frantically. When the whites of his eyes grew larger than his irises, Jinlei knew that he recognized them and their surroundings.

Wang Bai ripped the tape from his mouth, and he gave a cry of pain. He rested his eyes on Wang Bai and gave a mirthless laugh.

"Long time no see. Mother."

XVII

J inlei, Chains and Gidget all gaped at Wang Bai, as they stood around their captive.

"Mother?" Jinlei sputtered.

Wang Bai only shrugged a response.

The Chemist sat bound on a chair in the middle of the computer room. He blinked as he took in his surroundings. The large monitor to his right showed surveillance feeds, and he scoffed in understanding. "Same old place, I see. So, what? Is this where you plan your little operations? Your master plan of how to take me down?"

Wang Bai shrugged again. "Pretty much."

The Chemist laughed contemptuously. "So now you got kids doing your dirty work?"

"Yes, imagine that. Mere kids taking down the great Chemist," Wang Bai said sarcastically.

The Chemist nodded toward Jinlei. "So you finally found her."

Wang Bai snuck a quick glance at Jinlei. "It certainly appears so."

"Me?" Jinlei raised an uncertain finger to point at herself.

The Chemist raised his eyebrows questioningly, then laughed, turning to his mother. "Look at you, leading a lamb to her slaughter.

How did you find her anyway?"

"She found *me*."

"Whatever are you talking about?" Jinlei finally had it, putting her hands on her hips, demanding an answer.

"There's been an old saying passed down through our generations. Watch out for a girl who's a crane that turns into an eagle. My mother and her mother's mother and so on always told us to help this girl when we find her, for she is a lost soul, traveling in an unknown world. I still had my doubts when I sent you, but when I saw how you defeated my son, all doubts were erased."

"Because of my signature attack, 'Crane Turns to Eagle,'" Jinlei gasped. Her aunt must have passed along the message to her descendant and her descendant's descendant, and so on. They were instructed to help her should they ever encounter her. Her heart warmed at the thought.

Wang Bai continued, "Since the Hu family was trained in the southern Flying White Crane style of kung-fu because of a teacher who happened to be traveling around here in the north, that technique has been passed down for generations."

Jinlei nodded excitedly. "But I see you've added some modern techniques into it."

"Yes," Wang Bai acknowledged. "But family legend says there was a technique that could be used against the Flying White Crane. Unfortunately, it was lost before its inventor could write it down."

"That's me!" Jinlei exclaimed, hardly believing how her own lore could have survived this long. She marveled and thought proudly of her family's resilience.

The Chemist scoffed. "So now that you've fulfilled one family obligation, you're trying to rope me back in? When are you going to give up on me, my dear old mother?"

It was the first time Jinlei saw a break in the old woman's rigid mask of impassiveness.

"I will never give up on you. My son," Wang Bai said, still having her stoic bearing but with slightly moistened eyes.

Wang Bai's words had an adverse effect on the Chemist as he bellowed angrily, trying to wriggle himself out of the ropes. "Let me go," he said dangerously low.

"Not until you behave," Wang Bai said as if scolding a small child.

"So, what? You plan to keep me tied up here forever?"

"Yes. If you continue to misbehave." A mocking smile spread on her lips, typical of the stone-hearted Wang Bai they came to be familiar with.

The Chemist screamed out again, violently trying to break free from his restraints. But Wang Bai had tied the ropes too tightly.

Wang Bai remained calm, unfazed by her own son's hysterics. "It seems I won't be able to reason with you today. I'll come back tomorrow. In the meantime, you think about what you've done."

Jinlei, Chains and Gidget followed Wang Bai out of the room. Wang Bai turned off all the lights and shut the door. She locked the door with the facial recognition scanner, ensuring no one but her could open the door.

Jinlei shuddered, hearing the Chemist's disembodied screams as they left the dark basement behind them.

Chains muttered under his breath, "Remind me never to cross this old woman."

Gidget whispered back, "You're not her son. I think you're safe."

Once they were up the stairs and back in the store, Jinlei turned to Wang Bai. "We got you what you asked for. Now will you tell me how to find my mother's magic?"

Wang Bai relented. "Yes. Find Li."

"What?" After all the preparation and almost killing herself over Wang Bai's wishes, that was it? Her bones ached, and her eyes drooped from exhaustion. It was all Jinlei could do to stop herself from wringing Wang Bai's neck.

"That was the only clue as to how to find your mother's magic—passed down from Auntie Ying herself," Wang Bai explained.

Jinlei frowned in thought. *It certainly was a start*, she thought, too tired to argue with Wang Bai.

"Come back tomorrow," said Wang Bai. "I think I have a way to help you find out more."

* * *

The next day, they all slept until past noon. Jinlei stretched her arms and let out a satisfied groan, lazily blinking open her eyes. The long sleep did wonders for her brain, as she woke up instantly knowing what Wang Bai's clue meant.

At the café, Jinlei explained to them her theory. "Li must be referring to Jun's family. Since they were so close to our family, they must know something about my mother's magic." She turned to Gidget. "Could we do that thing you did again and try to find the Li descendants?"

"Of course." Gidget grinned.

They went to the market to get another DNA testing kit, then headed to Wang Bai's shop. When they arrived, Wang Bai turned the shop sign from 'Open' to 'Closed.'

"It's feeding time anyway," Wang Bai said.

They all followed Wang Bai down to the basement as she carried a tray of food. The Chemist looked even worse than yesterday, with large bags under his eyes and his face red from, Jinlei presumed, screaming the entire night.

Wang Bai shoveled a spoonful of rice and meat and tried feeding the Chemist, but he refused. He kept turning his head from side to side. It would have been the most natural thing in the world—a mother feeding her son—if her son wasn't a middle-aged man who was a criminal mastermind. Jinlei found it hard to watch. Chains found it amusing, chuckling under his breath. Gidget just looked bored.

Finally, Wang Bai gave up and set the tray on the floor. She took a seat and faced them all, sitting in their respective seats by the monitors.

"I asked you back here because I think we can continue our— shall we say, mutually beneficial relationship," Wang Bai began.

"You said you can help us find out more about the magic?" Jinlei asked.

"Yes." Wang Bai sat back, crossing her arms. "I can give you all the resources you need—computers, equipment, people, even a place to stay, so you don't have to keep staying at that ratty old hostel."

Jinlei narrowed her eyes at the crafty old woman. "What's the catch?"

"No catch. We just simply want you to go back to the past before all this happened."

"We?" Jinlei's eyes narrowed even further.

The Chemist let out a scornful chuckle.

Wang Bai was unfazed, smiling mysteriously. "I didn't tell you this before, but I'm part of a certain group of people who have a vested interest in bringing down the evils of this world."

"What group? And what people?" Jinlei shrunk back in her seat doubtfully.

"We don't really have a name. We're a loose group of individuals acting in concert."

"What she means is," the Chemist interrupted, "she's part of a secret organization hoping to bring down Corp. X using any means necessary." He laughed derisively. "And here she says I'm a criminal mastermind. I guess you're only a criminal if you're not on her side."

"There's a big difference between taking down a corrupt organization and wilfully creating sub-humans for nothing more than financial gain," Wang Bai retorted sharply.

The Chemist sneered. "Careful. If you join her, you're essentially joining a criminal organization. We don't want that, do we?"

Ignoring him, Wang Bai continued, "As my dear old son said, it is a secret organization involved in covert operations against Corp. X. As to the legality or illegality of our acts, well, that's debatable, and there is hardly evidence to prosecute anyone. The cops won't know the first place to look. They don't even know we exist. No one knows how far our networks go, but I assure you—our tentacles reach as wide as the ocean."

It all made sense to Jinlei. It explained how Wang Bai knew so much, why she had this secret basement, and how she could gather information no one else would be able to.

"Wait a minute . . ." Chains said, gazing suspiciously at Wang Bai, "Was that the reason you sent us to the auction? To see what we could do and recruit us? Was that some sort of audition?"

Wang Bai cocked her head nonchalantly. "Yes. You got a problem with that?"

Chains shrugged and flexed his muscles. "Not really. I need a good workout once in a while. Better you than Corp. X, I guess."

Gidget snapped her fingers. "Were you behind the massive outage on their internal servers last year?"

Wang Bai smiled proudly.

Gidget whooped and slapped her knees like an excited puppy. "That was genius! It completely incapacitated their operations. It took them days to go back online, and they lost over ¥500 million in revenue. How did you do it? How did you get past all their firewalls and redundancies?"

"We didn't," Wang Bai said. "It was the fault of a clueless intern who applied an incorrect configuration setting that disrupted their whole network by accident. He was fired, of course, but he's currently not unemployed, I'll tell you that."

Gidget laughed appreciatively. "That's what they said on the news—that it was an intern's fault. We suspected it really was a cyber attack, and the intern was just a scapegoat. I guess both are true."

The Chemist scraped his chair as he laughed derisively at Gidget. "What a naïve lot you are. They barely made any damage. Corp. X would have made that money back in a day. What have your tentacles really accomplished?" He turned to his mother. "You're nothing but a small fry in an ocean full of sharks. When are you going to learn there's no use fighting them? If you're smart, you would have done the same thing as I did and joined them instead."

"You're right," Wang Bai acknowledged. "Nothing we've done so far has done any serious damage on Corp. X's operations. We've only been minor irritants at best. But now everything's different. Now we have her." She cocked her head toward Jinlei.

"Me?" Jinlei asked uncertainly.

"Yes. If you do manage to travel back in time and kill the demon Dao Fei before he becomes the monster he is now, then we can prevent this miserable future from happening. We can prevent Corp. X's rise to the top."

"So Dao Fei is still alive?" Jinlei shook her head. The thought of him surviving a thousand years sent shudders throughout her body.

"Well, he hasn't been seen in decades," admitted Wang Bai. "But we presume he still is very much so. There's a darkness that permanently blankets this city, a constant sense of avarice and depression. The greed keeps growing, and more and more people, businesses, even whole countries are submitting to Corp. X. You could argue it's simply their shrewd business tactics that make them grow stronger. But it's more than that. There've been countless business rivals who have mysteriously disappeared. Young maidens seen going into Corp. X's forbidden inner chambers and never coming back out. And whispers of ritualistic sacrifices." She rubbed her temples. "For so long, our enemies have been much stronger. We've lost countless men and women in this fight. Some even turned to join the other side." She gave a side look to her son. "We couldn't continue to stand by and do nothing. But now everything's different."

Wang Bai's enigmatic eyes bore into Jinlei's as if putting all her hopes into one person. "For the first time, we finally have hope."

Jinlei gulped. Hope—that was far too heavy a burden to place on one person, let alone a young girl.

But even the Chemist remained silent.

Still, it was Jinlei's aim all along, wasn't it? She wanted to go back in time to help her family defeat Dao Fei. Nothing had changed for her.

"Well, what are we waiting for? Let's get me back to the past!"

XVIII

The Chemist still refused his food until the end, but he remained silent the rest of the time until they left. Jinlei thought his inner beast had softened a little.

Jinlei, Chains and Gidget went back to their hostel to gather their belongings and check out. Afterward, they met Wang Bai back at her shop. Wang Bei led them to an apartment building a few blocks down the street and gave them the keys to their new apartment. It wasn't much, but it was much better than the animal hovel masquerading as accommodations they'd been staying at. The whole apartment, as well as the furniture and amenities were simple and functional. In the kitchen and living room, there was a table that seated four and a black couch facing the television. They each had their own rooms, which all looked similar, with one single bed, a small table and a closet. They would all share a bathroom.

Wang Bai even bought Gidget a new high-powered computer with the fastest internet speed. Gidget could barely contain her excitement as she cracked her knuckles, waiting to test out her new toy.

Wang Bai left them to settle in. They all unpacked what meager belongings they had, and Gidget set up her new computer.

Jinlei and Chains sat on Gidget's bed as Gidget finished setting up and rebooting her computer. "Do you have anything that may contain Jun's DNA?" Gidget asked, not looking up from her computer. "Anything he's touched, anything he's given you?"

Jinlei patted herself down, trying to think. Then she remembered she was no longer wearing her old-fashioned clothes. She went back to her room and took her old robes which she hung in the closet. She handed Gidget her unwashed, blood-spattered clothes.

"Would this work?" Jinlei asked. Since she was standing so close to Jun when they were fighting Dao Fei, she was quite sure some of the blood wasn't hers.

"That's perfect! *Er*, do you mind if I cut off the piece with the blood?"

Jinlei's face fell. It was yet another of her personal belongings, her only links to the past that would be taken away. But she knew she had no choice. "Alright," she grumbled.

Gidget cut off a piece with a large blood stain, placed the sample onto the portable DNA tester's sample port. They had a few hours until the results, so they decided to buy some groceries.

They walked around for a bit, played a few games at the arcade, then went to the grocery store. All the while, Jinlei had the peculiar feeling of being watched, but every time she looked around, there was no one there. She hoped there wouldn't be another visit from the angry 'gods of time.'

When they got home, Gidget made dinner for them since, apparently, nobody else knew how to cook. Really, Gidget was like the heart of this operation. Sure, Jinlei and Chains could take down a couple dozen guys at once or leap off a building, but if it wasn't for Gidget, Jinlei wondered how they could survive this world.

Once the DNA testing was done, Gidget went to work on

her computer, and she was off to her own version of space-time travel where no one could reach her.

Gidget was slumped in front of her computer for hours, not talking, not eating, not drinking. She was like a living, reanimated corpse. In the meantime, Chains showed Jinlei how to work the television.

For a while, Jinlei was as spellbound as Gidget. She found her face growing numb from not blinking and her mouth remaining half-open for hours. Every time Chains pressed a button, the flashing box showed different scenes and different people. The screen filled up half the wall, and the pictures were so lifelike that she felt like she could almost touch them. Chains even showed her a feature where the pictures leaped out of the screen itself and played out as if they were actually in the living room. Chains called it a 'hologram.' The holographic images frightened her so, and she asked Chains to put them back in the box.

Some were well-dressed men and women in suits talking about the current state of the country. Some sang and danced, which Jinlei found fascinating. Some were young people clad in embarrassingly bare clothing, participating in matchmaking sessions. Jinlei flushed hot and asked Chains to press the button. Finally, they settled on a historical drama marathon. Jinlei pointed out all the inaccuracies she spotted but still felt much joy in the illusion of being back in her own time.

When the commercials came on, Jinlei welcomed the break as she stretched out on their sofa. "I don't get it. You can have all these modern conveniences in your own home. Why even bother to go outside?"

Chains chuckled. "Congratulations. You are now experiencing the plight of the modern man."

Somehow, Jinlei felt sad for them, even though she had thoroughly enjoyed herself.

They heard Gidget suddenly jump up from her chair and exclaimed, "I got it!"

Jinlei and Chains immediately went over to Gidget's room. "You found the Li descendants?" asked Jinlei.

"One. A John Doe." Gidget's smile immediately disappeared. "It's the same story as your family. Most of the clan was killed off during the Water Drop Rebellion. But I found one DNA match. Brace yourself."

"Show me," Jinlei said, waiting in anticipation.

"Here." Gidget showed them her findings on the screen. "There was a police incident report a few days back. Apparently, some guy had attacked a few Corp. X soldiers. They tried arresting him, but he escaped. It was all caught on camera."

Gidget played the clip. The footage showed a man in traditional Tang dynasty robes fighting with the Corp. X soldiers and police.

"That's Jun!" Jinlei screamed at the camera, hardly believing her eyes.

Miraculously, Jun managed to avoid the soldiers and police's modern weapons as he fought with his sheathed sword. There were only four assailants against him and he easily escaped once he saw a chance.

"I can't believe he made it here too." Jinlei was shaken with shock. "We have to find him right now!"

"It's already late. It's way past midnight," Gidget reasoned. "We can find him in the morning."

Jinlei shook her head adamantly. "No, we must find him this instant! He must be having a time of it, wandering the streets alone." She started to tremble, thinking about how lonely and confused he must be, all alone in this strange new world. She started to feel guilty, having met Chains and Gidget, who took very good care of her. And now Wang Bai, who even provided them a warm place to stay.

"Gidget's right," Chains said gently. "Besides, he must have found a place to sleep and hide at night. It will be hard to find him now."

Jinlei chewed her lip. She knew they were right. Jun was a smart one. He would have found a place to rest and retire. After some hemming and hawing, she finally gave in to Gidget and Chains's reasoning.

Jinlei tossed and turned in her bed all that night. As soon as day broke, she jumped from her bed, raring to face the day and go find Jun. She could hardly imagine what it would be like to see him here under the circumstances.

"Where should we start looking?" Jinlei asked Gidget.

"Thankfully, the police report was filed at Xiahe District, right across the river."

"Around Corp. X headquarters, where the Xia family used to live." Jinlei nodded in understanding.

They walked around Corp. X headquarters, where the footage of Jun took place. Up and down the river, the central square, the little alleyways and bootleg shops, they scoured the whole area. They showed people a still photo of Jun taken from the surveillance camera, asking them if they'd seen anyone who may look like him. Some yelled aggressively at them. Some tried to sell them bootlegs. Most brushed them off, walking off as if they hadn't heard anything.

"This is impossible," Jinlei said, wiping the sweat off her brow. "Is there any other way to look for him? Surely, with all the modern marvels of your technology, there would be an easier way to locate him?"

"I just thought of something," Chains said, scratching his chin.

Both Jinlei and Gidget raised their eyebrows doubtfully. Chains was hardly the idea person. He was more of the muscle.

Sensing their incredulity, he took offense at their lack of faith. "Yeah, I get ideas too." He shrugged. "The old lady says she has networks everywhere. Maybe she could help us? Isn't that what she said she was for anyway?"

Jinlei and Gidget looked at each other, hardly believing that they hadn't thought of the obvious before.

"He's right," Jinlei said.

They decided to go back to Wang Bai's shop when the hairs on Jinlei's back rose up again. The feeling of being watched.

She turned around, scanning the sea of people, buildings and cars. There. In the middle of the crowd. A street urchin was staring straight at her, the aura of black and purple emanating from his tattered clothes.

"We have to get out of here," Jinlei alerted the other two.

"We gotta lead him to where there are not much people," Chains said, his stance ready to bolt at any moment.

"In the back alley. Over there." Gidget gestured back to where they came from.

Jinlei nodded. "Alright. Ready? One . . . Two . . . Now!"

As the lights of the crosswalk turned to green, they exploded into a run across the street, toward the two buildings right next to each other, into the narrow alleyway between them.

The street urchin followed them all the way into the alley, and without stopping, Jinlei immediately turned to face him. She leveraged the walls on either side of her, stepping upward and forward until she landed behind him. The street urchin could barely process what was happening as Jinlei had him in a chokehold from behind. She touched pressure points on his back and neck, and he instantly fell unconscious.

Jinlei gently propped him up against the wall. She should have been relieved, but the strange sensation of being watched didn't go away. She turned around, ready for another fight.

And she saw then what—or who—had been stalking her.

The mysterious red-haired stranger.

"Chains. Gidget. Go find Jun. I'll meet you back at Old Wang's."

"Hey, you don't need to face him alone. Or leave him to me." Chains enthusiastically punched a fist into his palm.

But Jinlei knew it was her he was after and there was no sense delaying the inevitable fight. "No," she declared. "Besides, it shall be nighttime soon and it shall be harder to find Jun. Please find him for me. I won't take long."

"Alright," Gidget reluctantly agreed. "But here. So we can keep track of you."

Gidget removed her e-watch and put it on Jinlei. "Answer it when it rings, okay?"

Jinlei nodded.

With Chains and Gidget gone, Jinlei and the mysterious stranger faced off each other, waiting but ready for someone to make the first move.

"You've been following me, haven't you? How did you find me?" she demanded.

"I placed a tracker on you."

Jinlei's mind went back to their last fight when he cupped his hand on her neck. Was that when he had placed the tracker? But she hadn't felt or noticed anything strange on herself since then.

He smirked. "Lucky for me, you don't seem to hop in the shower all that much."

Jinlei fumed and leaped at him. He blocked easily with his arms. She followed through, blow by blow, one after the other. He blocked them easily, danced with her with his fancy footwork until he tripped her up. He caught her and, like last time, wound her arms behind her and trapped her legs between his. He smirked, his eyes shining like a wild animal who caught his prey.

He was toying with her. Which only infuriated Jinlei more. She butted her head against his nose as before.

"AH!" he cried, quickly letting go of her.

"I did 'hop in the shower,' as you say. Why didn't it come off?"

Still holding his nose, he said, "It's made with bio-compatible adhesion. It doesn't come off easily."

Jinlei didn't understand half of what he just said. She asked angrily, "How do I get it off then?"

After the stranger wiped the blood off his nose, he said, "If you just pick at it, it should come off."

Jinlei reached at the back of her neck. Sure enough, she felt a slight lump that she hadn't noticed before—not even when she was in the shower. She felt its edges and peeled it off with her nails. She studied it, trying to make sense of it. All she could make of it was that it was small and the color of her skin with mystifying blinking lights. She threw it on the floor and ground it up with her shoe.

"Why do you want to come after me?" she asked.

For a moment, he looked baffled. "You came after *me* first."

"That's because you were trying to kill that man when I saw you in the alley."

The stranger chortled sardonically. "That man is the head of Corp. X's R&D branch in Xiahe City and a relative of the Xias."

Jinlei stiffened. "Be that as it may, nobody deserves to die."

"Some do," he said with no emotion.

Jinlei's blood curdled within her. "How could you say such a thing?"

"A little girl like you playing at this game will never understand.

I plan to bring down the Corp. X empire even if I have to do it with my own bare hands, one person at a time," he said, his eyes burning. Jinlei thought she could even see specks of red in his dark eyes.

"And is that why you're coming after me now? You want to get rid of me too?" Jinlei lifted up her nose at him and looked him down, even though he towered over her.

"Do you know how long I've been tracking him? Mr. Big Shot Su Hanjin is rarely without his bodyguards. The only exceptions are when he visits his mistress, who lives in Lao Cheng District. Those are the only times he dresses down and pretends like he's one of the people. That was my chance." His voice turned into a low growl. "My only chance. And you ruined it."

He cracked his knuckles. He was serious about fighting now. Jinlei put her hands up and moved her leg backward into a bow stance.

Like a fierce whirlwind, they both went at each other at the same time. Each matching the other's speed. It was like they were in perfect sync, knowing where the other would attack and fending it off at the right moment. No one had landed a hit yet, but one of them inexplicably went down—the stranger. And Jinlei right after.

Jinlei vaguely felt a needle sharply pierce her arm. She struggled against the drowsiness she felt, blinking against her blurry vision. Figures clad in black hovered in and out of focus. Then everything went black.

XIX

Jinlei squinted against the bright lights. She blinked the blinding glare away, and slowly, her surroundings came into focus.

At first, she couldn't fathom where she was. She was bathed in white lights and surrounded by white walls, as if she was in empty space. There seemed to be another person lying down across from her. Slowly she stood up, still dazed. She tried walking across, toward the person lying down but found she couldn't go a step further as a glass barrier entrapped her within its four walls. She was enclosed in a glass cage.

She banged against the glass and put her whole weight against it, but it was as thick and strong as a concrete wall.

"Hello?" she called out. "Where am I? Who's out there?"

The answer came in a tapping sound beside her. She gasped and scrambled over to the side.

The mysterious stranger was also trapped in a glass cage beside her. She looked all around and realized the whole room was filled with glass cages with people inside. The room stretched out as far as her eyes could see.

"Where are we?" she yelled against the glass.

"Corp. X," the mysterious stranger answered.

"Why did they take us? What are they going to do?" she asked, her voice rising in a panic.

The mysterious stranger shrugged indifferently. "Who knows."

Jinlei couldn't believe how calm and unconcerned he was. "But what about all these people? How can they keep so many people here?"

The mysterious stranger smiled contemptuously. "And here, you wanted to spare Su Hanjin. I'll bet you anything he's behind all this."

Jinlei bared her teeth at him. She hardly thought this was the time to be pointing fingers at anyone. Besides, she stood by her beliefs. She wouldn't stand by and let anyone be cruelly executed, at least not in front of her.

She wondered how she was going to get out of this predicament now. Then she remembered. Gidget's watch. She looked down on her wrist, and to her shocking dismay, it was gone.

Seeing her look at her wrist, the mysterious stranger said, "They probably took it. They don't want anyone tracking you. My phone's gone too."

Jinlei sank to the floor. She was in completely unfamiliar surroundings. These cages were nothing like the wooden cages of old. If she was back home, she could break out of those wooden cages in no time.

"But how could these modern glass materials be so sturdy?" she asked the stranger.

The stranger rolled his eyes at her, not knowing why she was so ignorant about such things. "That's because it's probably reinforced with advanced polymers, making it unbreakable."

Jinlei scowled at him. "Well, if you're so smart, tell me how we can break out of this?"

The stranger's one eyebrow shot up. "We?"

Jinlei flushed. She didn't know why she said 'we' either. It might be because they were taken together. It seemed reasonable for them to help each other against a common enemy. At least for the time being. And she told him as much.

"The way I see it, it only makes sense for us to work together. At least for now. I mean, think about it." Jinlei moved closer to the glass. "It would be much easier to defeat dozens of guards with two people instead of one, do you not think so?"

The mysterious stranger remained quiet. But Jinlei could tell the wheels in his head were turning. Surely, it would be prudent for him to see things her way for once.

"You can continue to fight me—and lose—once we're out," Jinlei concluded, dangling the final blow that she knew he wouldn't be able to resist. She knew he would agree, if only for the sheer satisfaction of punishing her by defeating her after being insulted. It's what would have motivated her.

The stranger shrugged her off gruffly. "Fine." He faced away from her, scowling.

Jinlei smiled triumphantly. Then regarded him curiously. "What should I call you? I mean, now that we're sort of working together," she added quickly.

"Kai," he said without so much as a glance at her.

She nodded and hugged her knees in comfort. She didn't know why she felt a small victory in knowing the stranger's name and winning him over to her side. Sometimes, her competitive streak emerged at the unlikeliest of times.

"So, how do you propose we get out of this?" she asked again. It made sense to her to ask him for ideas since he probably had a better understanding of Corp. X's operations than she could ever have.

"The guards or other personnel might come to check on their

prisoners from time to time. That's our window. We get them to open our cages and fight our way out of here."

Jinlei leaned back, satisfied. At least they had a plan.

They continued to sit in silence, Jinlei pondering the strange turn of events in her life. How, just a few weeks ago, she had been in the comfort of her home. And within minutes, traveled far ahead into the future. And now, she was trapped in a glass cage, in a brightly lit room that was strangely the most depressing room she'd ever been in.

Sad wails of hopelessness drifted up and down the hallway from time to time. Most of the time, the patrons inside the cages seemed to have given up, slumped in the insides of their cells. Jinlei vowed never to give in to the oppression of this place, no matter how long it took to break out of here.

* * *

In this empty space filled with empty people, Jinlei didn't know how many minutes, hours or days had passed. She passed the time by trying to make conversation with the only person she knew.

Since their capture, she had gotten to know Kai a little bit, though he was still very much the mysterious stranger to her. He was a man of few words and even fewer thoughts. That was because he mainly had one preoccupation in his life—to bring down Corp. X.

"Why do you want to bring down Corp. X so badly?" Jinlei asked him once. She understood why people wanted to bring down the vilest corporation in the world—her included. But Kai was almost as single-minded as her, and no one became that way unless there was a deeper, more personal reason.

Kai merely grunted in response, "Why not?"

"What did they do to you?"

"It's not what they did to me," Kai said. But he said nothing more after that.

"Well, whatever it is, they've done worse to me," Jinlei said.

Kai snorted and laughed.

Jinlei couldn't slap him, so she knocked on the glass between them instead.

"Please. A princess like you? What, did they stop producing your favorite lipstick, and now you hold a grudge?"

Jinlei's mouth fell open in shock. "How dare you? I'm as much a street urchin as you!"

"First of all, no one who's actually a street urchin calls themselves a street urchin." Kai lifted up the side of his mouth in that sneering smile of his.

"Fine." Jinlei huffed. Besides, she wasn't even a princess, she was the daughter of a magistrate, but she wasn't going to tell him that. "Then if you want to take down the whole corporation, why stay here? I heard the main office is in the capital."

"Because I need something here. After I'm done here, I will go to the capital."

That intrigued Jinlei. Perhaps whatever he knows could help her with Dao Fei. "What are they keeping here?"

"Nothing you need to know."

Jinlei grumbled. Talking to him was like talking to a large fortress.

The door to their prison opened, seizing Jinlei's attention. *Is it feeding time already?* she wondered. Their wardens visited them once a day to bring them food. It was the only contact they had with the outside world since they'd been imprisoned. That, and from time to time, security personnel would open selected cages and haul some people out. No one knew where they went or what Corp. X planned to do with them.

When Kai and Jinlei first saw the wardens, they implored their captors with much passion to open their cages, only for their pleas to fall on deaf ears. Jinlei had since given up trying to talk to their captors. But she hadn't given up hope of escape.

Once, she had tried to break out of her cage when a warden opened the small opening at the bottom of the cage, big enough to slip in a tray of food. There was a keypad and a fingerprint scanner attached to the cage's door handle that controlled the opening and closing of the door, including the small slot at the bottom of the cage. Once the warden slipped in the tray of food, Jinlei violently pulled on the warden's arm, slamming his head against the cage door in the process. She threatened to break his arm and asked him to let her out. But all that effort was futile as Jinlei received an electric shock through the glass cage itself within minutes. She let the warden go and was punished by not being given food the next day.

"I told you not to do it," Kai had told her after. She had earlier told him what she had been thinking. "They have cameras all over the place and temperature-controlled cages. The electric shock was no surprise." He had looked up at the cameras and chuckled ironically at them. "Well played."

The people who came in this time weren't their usual wardens, however. And they certainly didn't have trays of food.

Kai stood up, alert. His eyes met Jinlei's. It was another hauling. They both knew this might be their chance.

"Him. Her. Him . . ." What looked to be the head of the team pointed to selected cages.

Lastly, the head guard rested his eyes on Jinlei and said with a satisfied sneer, "Her." He turned to his men. "Alright, that's it! Haul them out!"

Jinlei looked wide-eyed at Kai. Their plan was to go out together. That was their best chance.

Kai growled, slamming his fists against the cage. "HEY! Hey, half-man!" he yelled, referring to the head of security's short stature.

The head of security stopped and slowly turned toward Kai.

"Whatever you got going on, I'm your man," said Kai.

The head guard scoffed at him and turned away.

Desperate to keep his attention, Kai continued banging on the cage and yelling, "Oh, come on! Whatever you plan to do with them, I'd make a better guinea pig. Think about it. Hey!" He banged the cage once more. "You want me to bend down for you? I'll help you get things from the top shelves. How's that?"

Irritated now, the head guard stomped over to Kai's cage. "I'd shut your smart mouth if I were you. Count yourself lucky that you get to live another day. We have all the people we need." He stared Kai up (because Kai was too tall).

For a moment, it seemed that Kai would back down, then he said, "You sure you're not a little *short*?"

The head guard slammed Kai's cage with both hands. He yelled at the other guards, "I changed my mind. Not her. Him."

The guards were about to open Jinlei's cage but opened Kai's instead.

"Wait!" Jinlei pleaded. "Please! Let me out too!"

But the guards didn't give a second look back and neither did Kai, as they all marched out the room. The door slammed shut. Everything was quiet once again.

Jinlei collapsed to the floor, losing hope for the first time.

* * *

Jinlei didn't know how long she had been staring up at the white ceiling. She wondered if Kai managed to escape. If he did, then he must have abandoned her, she thought bitterly. She had to think of another way to break herself out of there. She didn't know how much longer she could take being confined in a small box, constantly blinded by white lights.

The door opened again, and Jinlei sat up. Maybe this was the chance she was hoping for.

She gasped when she saw who was coming toward her.

"Chains?" she whispered.

Chains was dragging an unconscious man with him.

"We don't have much time," Chains said through the glass.

Chains entered the code and pressed the unconscious man's fingerprint on the scanner to open the cage door.

"Let's go," Chains urged.

Jinlei had so many questions, but she knew now wasn't the right time to ask them. They furtively ran out the door, into the white hallway, which didn't look all that different from the white prison from which Jinlei emerged.

"Where to, G?" Chains whispered into his lapel.

From Gidget's instructions, Chains led them to the end of the hall. They went through the emergency exit, and Chains proceeded to climb up the stairs.

"Wait!" Jinlei hissed at Chains. "Are you sure this is the way out?" She didn't know much about modern architecture, but she was fairly certain that the way out would be down the stairs.

"No. We have to go to the experimental lab," Chains replied.

"Why?"

"Because we have to find Jun."

XX

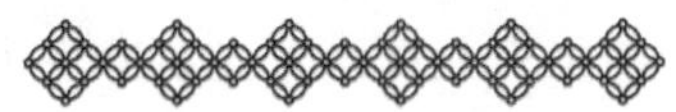

"Jun?" Jinlei hissed at Chains.

"Ironically enough, we found him when we were looking for you," Chains explained as they continued running up the stairs. "When we didn't hear back from you after a few hours, we kept trying to call Gidget's watch, but you weren't picking up. Gidget tracked the last known location of her e-watch, and it was somewhere around Corp. X's building. We figured you must have gotten taken somehow."

They ran a few more flights of stairs, neither of them out of breath yet.

Chains continued, "Gidget and Old Wang hacked the security cameras around the area and inside the building and saw you and that guy being carried inside. Looked like you were unconscious. We also happened to see Jun being taken in the same way."

Finally, they reached their destination. Chains checked with Gidget if the hallways were clear. Gidget did her magic and temporarily disabled the surveillance cameras in the hallway.

Before Chains opened the door, he added, "Old Wang also instructed us to find the Chemist's briefcase and destroy whatever files they made from it."

"Files?" Jinlei asked.

"It may be a long shot, but hopefully, Corp. X hasn't had a chance to dig into what was inside the briefcase. Even if they have, we can still take the original files and destroy what remaining records they have. Gidget will talk me through how to hack through their systems," Chains said before gingerly opening the door.

Chains listened to Gidget's instructions through his ear. They went down the hallway and made a right to a door with a nameplate that read, 'Head Scientist.' The door was locked, but Chains placed his eye in front of the security retinal scanner and the door unlocked. Jinlei looked at him in wonder.

He whispered, "That's why it took so long to get you. We had to plan to get past the security features. This little baby—" he pointed to his eyes, "—augmented contact lenses that mimic the eyes of Su Hanjin, the head honcho of this whole building. It took us a while to get. Let's just say I had to finesse his secretary a little bit." He winked at her.

Jinlei had an inkling what kind of finessing Chains had to do with the secretary. "That must have been so hard for you," Jinlei retorted sarcastically.

They shut the door silently behind them, and Chains got to work on the computer. "Alright, G. Tell me what to do."

Chains clacked away on the computer while Jinlei tried to decipher what was going on in front of her. The screens moved too quickly from one window to the other, and sometimes the text was just lines of gibberish. The unrecognizable figures danced in front of Jinlei, making her cross-eyed. She closed her eyes and shook her head, forcing herself to concentrate. She didn't know how, but she felt she should pay attention in case she could help.

Finally, it seemed that Chains located the so-called files he was looking for. He murmured as he scanned the words. He looked just as confused as her.

"What is it?" Jinlei asked.

With knitted eyebrows, Chains said, "Apparently, the briefcase Su Hanjin stole from the Chemist contained some kind of drug called the Diablocyte-X. This is the formula and lab report."

Jinlei and Chains looked at each other and shrugged. Even though it was written in Chinese, it may as well have been a foreign language. Chains apparently thought the same. Without further ceremony, Chains pressed a key, and the words disappeared. He deleted all the files associated with the drug.

"Now, we look for Jun," Chains said as he shut down the computer. "Apparently, there's a research and experimental lab on this floor where they experiment on their kidnapped victims. That should also be where the briefcase is."

Waves of anger and worry washed over Jinlei as she thought of Jun and how close she had come to being experimented on. "You mean they're experimenting on people with the drug they stole? What does the drug do?"

"I know about as much as you," Chains said.

They made their way out of the hallway again, ensuring no one was around and only moving when Gidget told them it was safe.

They headed to the very end of the hall, where a large room with walls made of glass loomed in front of them. Even at a late hour, there were still men and women in long white coats milling about the computers and observing the specimens—humans they had collected and strapped onto a bed.

They quickly ducked into a corner before anyone could see them.

"What do we do? There's nowhere to hide in that room. And

it's filled with people," Jinlei whispered harshly.

Chains looked around him, thinking. "There was a supply closet back there. We should find some lab coats to blend in. Once we're in there, you go find Jun. I'll find the briefcase. Hopefully, we can sneak out without anyone noticing."

"But we'll fight if we have to," Jinlei said out loud what they were both thinking.

"Yeah. Luckily, I don't think any of those guys will put up much of a fight. But we have to be ready when the guards come."

Chains and Jinlei made their way back down the hallway to the supply closet, where they got their white lab coats.

Chains's augmented contact lenses granted them access to the research lab. One or two people regarded them in surprise, probably because of Chains's dyed yellow hair. He fit in about as well as a Tang dynasty noble in a high-tech future. He casually nodded and greeted them, moving about as if he belonged.

Jinlei had to hand it to Chains—what he lacked in subtlety, he made up for in confidence. She followed along, walking past the computer monitors, when something caught her eye. She urgently tapped Chains's arm and pointed to the screen.

"Look. Isn't that the Chemist?" she whispered to Chains.

They both looked fixedly at the picture of the younger-looking Chemist and the accompanying text. It read: 'Personnel Files' and below it, 'Name: Wang Bo.'

"Wang." Jinlei turned to Chains.

"Same family name. He's Wang Bai's son, alright." Chains clucked his tongue.

Evidently, he was employed with Corp. X from the time he was a university student up until seven years ago. He steadily rose up the ranks, starting as an intern to a mid-level scientist, until he became the principal research scientist, heading the entire Future Biotechnological Engineering Innovation division. Below his brief biography were the projects he worked on.

"May I help you?" a voice sounding more like a warning than an offer of help startled Jinlei and Chains out of their fixation on the screen.

"*Er* . . . yeah, sorry. I just got distracted. I've heard of this guy. He was a legend around here, wasn't he?" Chains smoothly covered both of them.

"Yes, well," the young scientist sidled over in front of the screen. "His research was top-notch. The fundamentals of what he started still help our research to this day, but he wasn't a very good employee."

"Really? Why not?" Chains asked curiously.

"Well, for one thing, he just stopped showing up to work and disappeared off the face of the earth," the scientist said dismissively. "Is there a workstation you're assigned to?"

"Oh, yeah. Right over there." Chains chuckled as he casually strolled over to a blank computer screen.

Jinlei left Chains to do his part, and she quickly moved from the computer and research area of the room to the experimental area, where the research subjects were strapped onto rolling beds.

Jinlei avoided anyone's eyes and tried to emulate Chains, moving about as if she belonged. There were about ten men and women tied down on the beds while the people in the white coats discussed amongst themselves. She didn't see Jun among them, but the white coats were gathered around one particular person—Kai. He seemed to be in a deep sleep. There were things attached to him— wires leading to a monitor displaying confounding lines and emitting beeping noises at regular intervals.

Among the scientists observing Kai, there was one other man in a sharp suit instead of a white lab coat who stood out for his pompous aura of self-importance. There was an air of nervous obsequiousness among the people gathered around him. They hung onto his every word and tried to please him with their words. Jinlei recognized him as the man Kai was after—Su Hanjin.

Jinlei ducked her head, hoping Su Hanjin wouldn't recognize her from those nights at the auction and the café.

One of the women observed Kai, read from her tablet, and checked the monitor, announcing to the group, "He's a fine specimen, alright. All his vitals show exceptional results. He's young and healthy, the perfect subject."

A man nodded to another man in a coat, who brought out an apparatus with a needle. Jinlei surreptitiously inserted herself among the white coats, not calling attention to herself.

"Let's see how Specimen 60 reacts to the Chemist's formula," Su Hanjin said.

Before Jinlei knew it, the man jabbed the needle into Kai's arm. Kai violently awoke, thrashing and wrestling against his restraints. The monitor beside him beeped faster, showing the lines spiking up and down.

The men and women surrounding Kai looked on impassively. Su Hanjin's eyes danced in amusement, a little sneer of satisfaction formed on his lips. Others conferred with each other. Some continued to observe and write things down on their tablets.

The woman who spoke earlier studied the monitor, looked at her watch, then said, "No sign of reaction to the drug. Others started taking on visible symptoms by this time."

Kai roared with guttural, almost inhuman sounds, raging

savagely at the people around him.

The scientists continued to observe. Jinlei bit her lip anxiously and looked for Chains. When she saw that Chains had found the briefcase, she scanned the room for a way to free Kai. His restraints were made of thick, heavy metal, and there was no way Jinlei could simply tear it apart. She bit her lip as her eyes moved rapidly. From what she'd learned, many things in this modern world were operated by the touch of a button. There was a button on the side of the rolling bed. She prayed her suspicion was correct and pressed the button.

Within seconds, the metal straps restraining Kai opened up. He broke free and thrashed everything around him. The scientists howled in alarm. Kai showed them the same mercy they showed him. He first went for Su Hanjin, but the scientists threw themselves in front of Su Hanjin, and the executive was quickly ushered out to safety.

Kai was like a wild animal freed from his cage. He was set on his prey, hurling those who stood in his way across the room.

Somewhere in the room, loud alarm bells rang. Some were on the phones, calling for security.

Chains yelled for Jinlei. "We have to go! NOW!"

"Kai!" Jinlei yelled over the noise. "Come on!" She grabbed his arm and forcibly dragged him along with them.

As if coming back to his senses, the wildness in Kai's eyes appeared to subside, and he recognized Jinlei.

In the hallway, the alarm bells continued, emergency lights flashing in and out.

"G! Where to?" Chains talked into his lapel.

"We still have to find Jun!" Jinlei yelled over the blaring sirens.

"G?" Chains asked again.

Without a word, Kai went straight to the elevator where the

door just closed on him. He banged the doors in frustration, narrowly missing getting his hands on Su Hanjin.

"Kai!" Jinlei urged.

Kai growled. With no other choice, he followed Chains and Jinlei toward the emergency exit, the same one they had come from earlier.

Kai bounded up the stairs as Chains and Jinlei were about to go down.

"Kai!" Jinlei bellowed after Kai but he wasn't listening. "Chains! We can't leave him alone!" she called out to Chains as she started following Kai up the stairs.

"Why not?" Chains asked, as he too, doubled back and went up instead of down.

"He's going to kill Su Hanjin."

"So?" Chains said, with the same indifference as Kai.

"We can't let him do that!" Jinlei insisted. "Besides, we still have to look for Jun! Does Gidget know where they could be keeping him?"

"G?" After a pause, Chains said, "Well, what do you know? We are on the right path, after all. Gidget traced his whereabouts to the executives' floor."

"Let's go!" Jinlei urged Kai and Chains. They sprinted the rest of the way up the stairs.

When they reached the c-suite executives' floor, Chains led the way, following Gidget's instructions through his ear, until they reached large double doors made of African blackwood, gilded with real gold trimmings.

Chains opened the locked door with the retinal scan. All was deceptively quiet.

Su Hanjin's office had an outer and inner chamber. The outer chamber appeared to be a waiting room for visitors, with couches, snacks and a television screen. The secretary's desk was in this room too.

The nameplate on the door to the executive's inner chamber read, 'Su Hanjin.'

Chains gingerly opened the door, ready to fight whatever would have jumped out. But no one came at them. There was only one person in the room waiting for them.

"What took you so long?" Su Hanjin asked. He was eerily calm.

Kai let out a soft, animalistic growl under his breath.

"Xu Kai." Su Hanjin chuckled. "I always thought you looked familiar ever since our first encounter. I wondered why you were constantly after me. What could I have done to make you hate me so?" he said, his voice dripping with false sadness. "Then I found out it wasn't anything I'd done."

Su Hanjin straightened. He regarded Kai like his own personal experimental specimen. "Xu Kai. Son of Xu Ming. It seems like you still hold a grudge against your father. Really, if you wanted to get to your father, all you had to do was ask."

"It's not just my father. I'll bring down all of you if I have to tear this whole place down brick by brick with my bare hands," Kai said menacingly.

Su Hanjun laughed and applauded. "You're just as stubborn and tenacious as he is. It's a shame. All that talent misdirected. We could have made good use of you, just like we have of him. And look where he is now. Thriving. Powerful. Rich. You could have all that too. Instead, you're living in dirt, in some crowded shared room above a sewer."

Su Hanjin had a satisfied look on his face when Kai stiffened at the thought that Su Hanjin knew where he lived. "Ah yes," Su Hanjin said. "You're not the only one who's been doing some investigating."

Su Hanjin suavely leaned back against his desk. "I had hoped that the drug would have worked on you. I do have a proposition for you just because you're Xu Ming's son, and I see enormous potential in you. Join us, and all will be forgiven. Your first assignment," he nodded at Jinlei and Chains, "is to eliminate these two."

Jinlei snapped her head toward Kai. Surely he wouldn't betray them for him?

To her relief, Kai started to laugh.

Kai said, "Over my dead body."

Su Hanjin sighed dramatically. "You disappoint me once again. I had hoped it wouldn't come to this."

There were two more doors in Su Hanjin's inner office aside from the door from which they entered. He looked to the door on his right, then said, "Bring him out."

The door opened, and out came the monstrous hybrid of a human and demon, just like at the auction. He had tiny horns emerging from his head, a tail, grotesquely bulging muscles. But the most surprising thing of all was his face—there were traces of what used to be handsome, delicate features but warped into unnatural, sharp angles. It was a face Jinlei used to know.

"Jun," Jinlei gasped.

XXI

This time, it was Jinlei's turn to direct her venom at Su Hanjin. She lunged after him, but she was seized and thrown across the room—by Jun.

The impact rattled Jinlei. Her whole body throbbed with pain. But it didn't compare to the sting of Jun inflicting the pain on her. Her eyes clouded over, seeing Jun stalk over to her, ready to launch another attack. She was paralyzed with shock. In all her life, she never would have believed Jun was capable of ever hurting her.

Chains came just in time to block Jun's incoming fists.

In all the haze, Jinlei barely registered the influx of Su Hanjin's security into the room. Kai snarled at the uniformed guards, who kept him from getting his hands on Su Hanjin. He threw his fists and kicks like a wild beast. But with their modern weapons, the guards easily overpowered and outnumbered Kai. They shot at Kai with their stun guns, but the electric currents didn't seem to affect Kai, passing through his clothes like his clothes were armor themselves.

Su Hanjin thought ahead and didn't take any chances. A hovercraft hovered right outside his window. Su Hanjin stepped out of his large window to a waiting guard hanging from the hovercraft doors.

Before Su Hanjin safely latched onto the guard dangling from the hovercraft, he said, "I'm sorry it had to end this way, Xu Kai! Enjoy my latest creation! The semi-devil!"

Su Hanjin whisked away with the hovercraft, laughing all the while.

"Jinlei!" Chains called for Jinlei, raising her out of her stupor. "We need your help!"

Chains was barely holding on, taking the beatings from Jun. With his physiological enhancements, Jun was ten times stronger than Jinlei had ever seen him to be. Kai was still preoccupied with the guards.

Jinlei forced herself to stand up from the shock. They needed her.

The right moment came when Jinlei recognized Jun about to launch his signature attack—Flying Dragon Drives the Wind. It was an aggressive attack meant to force his opponent into a submissive position. Jun prepared to destabilize Chains by first pretending to yield to Chains's attacks. Then he would unexpectedly turn the tides.

Jun aimed for Chains's legs with a rush of successive, zig-zagged, sweeping techniques. Once Chains fell, Jinlei knew that Jun would attack from above to deliver the final, crushing blow. Before Jun could finish the fight, Jinlei leaped into action, flying toward him like a crane. She intercepted his Crushing Dragon Fist. Jun fell, momentarily impaired.

A stray electric bullet from one of the guards' guns came shooting at them. Thinking quickly, Chains picked up the fallen Jun, using him as a shield. The bullet completely stunned Jun into unconscious oblivion.

Jinlei screamed. "Jun!" She turned toward Chains with venom in her eyes.

Chains was unremorseful and moved on to help Kai battle the guards. With Chains and Kai together, they destroyed the guards in no time. Kai finished with a twist of a guard's neck, and Chains finished with a shattering blow to a guard's helmet.

"We've gotta get outta here. Now," Chains declared as soon as the last guard fell.

Jinlei barely heard Chains, still gripping Jun, frozen in fear at his unmoving body. Kai knelt beside them and checked for Jun's pulse.

"Don't worry. He's still alive. Whatever that damned Su Hanjin gave him enhanced his physical capacities," Kai said as he put Jun's arm around his neck and picked Jun up. "Let's go," he said in a no-nonsense manner. Jinlei knew it was the most practical and reasonable thing to do at the moment. Except she couldn't help but carry excess resentment toward Chains.

Ultimately, her rational side won, and she trailed after Chains, who followed Gidget's instructions in his ear.

Su Hanjin had a private elevator in his executive suite, inside the other locked door. Chains kicked open the locked door, revealing a large safe and a hidden panic room behind the safe with an elevator going straight down to the ground floor. They rode the elevator in strained silence.

They emerged at the back of the building to a black Corp. X van waiting for them.

Jinlei tensed, ready for another round of fighting. But the door opened, revealing Wang Bai in the passenger's seat and a driver Jinlei had never seen before.

"Get in. Quick," Wang Bai instructed. "Don't worry, he's one of my inside men at Corp. X," she explained, cocking her head at the driver.

They all filed in the back of the van, and the van drove off past the guards at the gates. No questions asked.

When they were safely a distance from the Corp. X building,

Jinlei asked, "Where's Gidget?"

"We're meeting her soon," Wang Bai replied.

Jinlei grunted an acknowledgement, still trying her best to ignore Chains and steaming about Jun, who was sprawled out in the very back of the van. She wanted to go over and hold him, stroke his hair and let him know everything will be alright. But such a blatant display of affection was unbecoming of a proper young lady. Especially in front of other people.

Soon, they rolled to a stop, arriving on a quiet street, just before the bridge to the other side of the river. An unmarked van was parked just beside them, the same unmarked van they used during the auction.

They all transferred from the Corp. X van to the unmarked van, where Gidget was waiting for them with all the outfitted computers and surveillance equipment.

"Thanks, Xiao Di," said Wang Bai as she got off the Corp. X van.

"Always at your service, Master Wang," said the driver before he drove away.

Wang Bai drove them all back to her shop.

* * *

They were all gathered in the basement of Wang Bai's shop. Wang Bai's basement had several other rooms, one of which was a sparse guest room of some kind with a bed, a nightstand and a closet. It also served as a storeroom for discarded items. Kai had Jun propped on his shoulder, and he laid Jun down on the bed. Wang Bai proceeded to tie Jun down with ropes.

Seeing Jinlei's horrified look at Jun being tied down, Wang Bai explained, "In case he wakes up and decides to go on a rampage."

Jinlei couldn't argue with that reasoning.

"Will he be alright?" Jinlei asked quietly.

"We'll have my son look after him. Come," Wang Bai said, leading them all to the computer room.

At the computer room, the Chemist, or who Jinlei now knew to be Wang Bo, was out of his restraints. He no longer looked like a madman and rather looked like a regular citizen. He was freshly showered and dressed in a new set of clothes.

Jinlei turned to Gidget, who was next to her, with a bewildered look.

Gidget explained, "He had an epiphany while you were away. He agreed to finally join his mother's side."

"What made you change your mind?" asked Jinlei.

Wang Bo grunted, and his mother answered for him, "When both you and Li Jun were taken, he realized the enormity of what could happen if both of you were harmed and unable to go back to the past. The fragile hope of bringing some relief to this world if we can send you both back to the past was threatened. My son won't speak to it, but I'm sure he felt the same as I did. He chose to hold on to hope."

Wang Bai gazed in awe at Jinlei, a break in her usually stoic mask.

"All the stories we've been told as children, stories passed down from one generation to the next, turned out to be true. When you're told stories as a child, you regard them merely as such—fairy stories of make-believe. Imagine what it must be like to witness a story come to life. It's a marvel like no other."

Jinlei looked away, unsure of how to feel. She was flattered at Wang Bai's high regard toward her but, at the same time, felt the immense weight of undue responsibility. It was one thing to strive for a goal of her own and quite another to have other people's enormous hope resting on her.

"But I'm still the Chemist. You can call me Chem from now

on," Wang Bo, or Chem, insisted like a petulant child.

Jinlei rolled her eyes. It didn't matter much to her what name he went by. She changed the subject. "What do we do about Jun? Is this your drug that did this?" she stared directly into Chem's eyes.

To her surprise, Chem didn't flinch but faced her head-on. "Yes."

"Then you know how to fix it," Jinlei said as more of a command than a statement.

Chem nodded. "You have my briefcase?"

Chains handed him the briefcase.

Chem's face fell when he opened it. "The formulas are still here, but they've taken all the samples. Including the samples for the antidote."

"Well, you can still make it, right? The formulas are still there, after all," Jinlei reasoned, trying to keep her voice from rising to a panicked pitch.

"Yes, but the ingredients are hard to get. Through the black market, it'll take weeks for the order to arrive from overseas. Synthetic chemicals and biological raw materials are highly regulated in this country, courtesy of Corp. X, of course. They're highly influential in government policies and ensure that industry policies enacted by the government benefit them. They've made sure they have a monopoly on the pharmaceutical business in this country and have restricted importations of synthetic chemicals for pharmaceutical use while they have easy access." Chem fixed his glasses on his face. "When I ordered the ingredients in the past, I had to go through extensive and convoluted networks to smuggle them in. But even if I do have the ingredients, it'll still take days, even a week, without proper equipment to engineer and cultivate the needed mammalian and demonic cells."

"Okay," Jinlei said, thinking quickly as she struggled to process all the information and science jargon Chem threw at her. "Then let's order the ingredients now. There's no time to waste."

But Chem merely looked at her with regret. "I'm afraid—if we don't want him to remain in this state forever, we have to give him the antidote. Fast. Or the drug will permanently alter his cells."

Jinlei steeled herself. "How long do we have?"

"About forty-eight hours from the time the drug was injected. Seventy-two hours, max. Depends on how well his antibodies fight the invading foreign agent." He looked on helplessly at Jinlei and shrugged in defeat. "Our best bet would be either to take the antidote from Corp. X, that is if they hadn't used it yet, or take the necessary ingredients from Corp. X."

Without hesitation, Jinlei said to Wang Bai, "Fine. Send me back in there."

Wang Bai stiffened as if preparing for an onslaught from Jinlei. "I don't think that's a wise idea. Their regional headquarters had just been attacked. They would be extra vigilant in the coming weeks. It's best to lay low for the time being."

Jinlei couldn't believe what she was hearing. She moved a dangerous step closer to both of them, the controlled rage evident in her whole bearing. "Listen here, you old hag and oily-haired fool. I've done everything you've asked. I've put my life on the line. You told me I was your only hope. And now you're telling me there's nothing we can do for Jun?"

Wang Bai was unruffled and said, "We never said there was nothing we could do. Just that it might be difficult to procure the necessary antidote for Jun."

"Fine," Jinlei said, daring the woman in front of her. "Do you have any suggestions on how we might get it?"

"I do." Wang Bai turned to the newest visitor to her secret

basement. "I don't think we've been properly introduced, young man. You are Xu Kai, correct?"

"Yeah," Kai said indifferently.

Wang Bai spoke and looked at him as if they were the same height instead of the little woman she was, only reaching below his shoulders. "We've tried to gather some information on you, but I must admit, we weren't entirely successful. You've succeeded in becoming a ghost, if that was your intention. Evidently, after tonight's operation, your aim was to kill Su Hanjin because you hold a grudge, correct?"

"Yeah," Kai said again. "Who are you people anyway? What's with all this?" He scowled at all the fancy equipment but didn't possess a hostile bearing, indicating he was more curious than suspicious.

Wang Bai smiled. "You'll be pleased to know we're fighting on the same side. We've been trying to take down Corp. X long before you even existed in this world. What if I told you, we can help you accomplish what you want?"

Kai squinted at Wang Bai with intense scrutiny. "What's the catch?"

Wang Bai's eyes glittered mysteriously. "No catch. We've been tracking Su Hanjin for weeks. I can say with confidence we know where he'll be in the next few days and when he'll be most vulnerable. What do you say?"

Kai forced a laugh. "No thanks, lady. I don't know what shady operation you got going on here, but I work alone."

Wang Bai still kept her unruffled bearing. "Oh, really? And how do you plan to catch Su Hanjin now that he knows about you and has most likely increased his security detail? Not to mention the guards who are probably hot on your tail now?"

Kai grunted. "It'll take some time, but I'll eventually get to him once things die down."

"And how long do you think that will take, huh? They've got endless resources. They can wait you out longer than you can wait them out. And the longer you wait, the harder it'll be to catch him."

Kai became silent, which emboldened Wang Bai.

"What if I told you, you can catch Su Hanjin as early as tomorrow?" Wang Bai's eyes glittered again, as if she was casting a spell.

Kai shifted. His interest was piqued. "How?"

Wang Bai smiled in triumph and crossed her arms. "So? Are you in?"

Kai pondered the question, looking around him at all the strange, expectant faces.

Jinlei noticed him rest his eyes on her longer than he did on the others. Jinlei stared back intently at him, communicating with invisible messages for him to join them. She knew he would get the job done no matter what. If they could get at Su Hanjin together, there was a higher likelihood of success. They would both get what they want. Kai would get his hands on Su Hanjin, and Jinlei would get the antidote.

Kai eased back his shoulders. "Fine. But only this once. Don't think I'm a part of your—whatever this is—for good."

"Of course not. Only this once." Wang Bai smiled.

Wang Bai turned to Jinlei, again assuming the role of commander. "I'll provide the logistics and any support for you and Kai to catch Su Hanjin. Once you have him, make him give you the antidote or, at least, the ingredients we need."

Still embittered, Jinlei found Wang Bai's air of authority grating, stoking the fires of her frustration. "Don't tell me what to do. Just make sure you actually do your job," she said as she stomped off.

XXII

Jinlei sat beside Jun's side. He was still unconscious but looked better than yesterday. Some color had gone back to his cheeks. Chem tended to him all night. An intravenous line connected to a bag of liquid medicine and nutrients was injected into Jun's arm, and Chem regularly checked his pulse and replaced the bag.

"He'll be fine," Chem assured Jinlei. "His semi-devil state grants him increased resilience and strength like a demon. He'll be awake in no time. Hopefully not before we administer the antidote."

Jinlei barely slept the night before back at their apartment, tossing and turning thinking about Jun and the upcoming ambush on Su Hanjin. In the morning, they all came back to Wang Bai's basement to discuss strategy. Jinlei still hadn't spoken to Chains since the incident with Jun. Chains hung back by the door, giving Jinlei space, while Gidget sat beside her.

Kai had slept in the basement in one of Wang Bai's other spare rooms. He was in the computer room with Wang Bai at the moment, looking through surveillance tapes of Su Hanjin's previous whereabouts.

After more assurances of Jun's condition, Jinlei followed the others to the computer room, where they overheard the tail end of

Wang Bai and Kai's conversation.

"What did I tell you? I was right," Wang Bai said.

Kai stared at the screen, crossed his arms, and agreed, "It appears so."

"What are you talking about? What's right?" Jinlei asked, taking a seat in front of a screen. Gidget sat beside her, and Chains and Chem stood behind them.

"Su Hanjin's whereabouts." Wang Bai played back footage over the past few weeks. "See? He's seen regularly going in and out of this apartment, though at different days and times so it's hard to predict when he'll visit next. But he visits at least three times a week."

Jinlei furrowed her eyebrows. "What's in this apartment?"

"His mistress," Kai replied.

"Why am I not surprised," Jinlei muttered. Concubines weren't unusual, even back home. That was at least a concept Jinlei was familiar with, though she didn't necessarily support it, especially since her father deliberately refused to take a concubine out of loyalty to her mother.

"It seems he's still taking precautions and avoiding set patterns," Wang Bai explained further. "He travels with four bodyguards. Two situated outside the building and two right outside the mistress's door."

Jinlei remembered the glamorous young lady at the café. *What could a fine young woman like her possibly want with a horrible brute like Su Hanjin?* she thought.

Wang Bai continued, "He's only visited once this week, so I'm thinking it's about time he shows up. Especially after the night he had—he's going to want to unwind."

Kai snickered contemptuously. "Doesn't matter how much precaution he takes. He's as predictable as any chump off the streets."

Wang Bai echoed Kai's sentiment with a derisive chuckle of

her own. "We're tapped into the surveillance cameras on the streets surrounding the apartment. As soon as we see him arriving, we move."

Chains punched a fist into his open palm. "Only four bodyguards? It'll be a piece of cake."

"You're not coming," Jinlei said icily.

Chains blinked. He was caught off guard that his mouth opened and closed without any sounds coming out. When he finally found his voice, he sputtered, "Why not?"

It was Jinlei's turn to regard him in surprise. "You know why! What if you use *me* as a human shield next time, huh?"

Chains's mouth hung open at the insinuation. "Come on! That was different, and you know it! Jun was a semi-devil. He would have been able to withstand the electric bullet."

Jinlei glared at him. "And you knew that when you threw him in front of that blasted thing?"

Chains scoffed. "No, of course not. But I had a hunch. And I was right! So it's all good!"

"No, it's not all good!" Jinlei objected, getting up from her seat to face Chains.

"Well, it should be. That gun was aimed at you. Would you rather I let you get fried alive?"

Jinlei stubbornly crossed her arms and shot daggers at Chains with her eyes.

Gidget tried to get in between them. "Come on, Jinlei. You know Chains wouldn't intentionally put Jun into harm's way, and he was only trying to protect you."

"Actually, Jinlei's right. Chains, you shouldn't go with them," Wang Bai piped in.

Chains gaped at her. Jinlei smiled in triumph.

Wang Bai laid out her plan, "Chains, you wait outside the building and act as backup. Don't let the outside guards go inside while Jinlei and Kai are in there."

"Alright," said Chains, relieved that he wouldn't just be sitting around.

Jinlei wasn't displeased with the plan. At least she wouldn't have to be around Chains.

They spent the rest of the day taking turns watching the surveillance cameras. Jinlei spent her time going back and forth between the computer room and Jun. Jun still wasn't awake yet, but he had started to stir.

Jinlei started to pace around anxiously. How much longer would they have to wait for Su Hanjin to show up? If Jun awoke before they got the antidote, they would have another problem to deal with. With Jun's strength as a semi-devil, the ropes wouldn't keep him tied down for long.

It was nearly midnight. Everyone was starting to get agitated and restless. Every time someone said something, it was met with an irate response.

The whole night passed with all of them only dozing off for a few hours.

* * *

The next day, Kai jumped up restlessly from his chair. "We can't just sit around like this," he declared.

"I agree," Jinlei said. "We only have a limited time to get the antidote for Jun."

"What do you suggest we do?" Gidget asked.

The wheels in Jinlei's head were turning quickly. "Is there any way we can for sure know when Su Hanjin will show up? Surely there's something in your newfangled technology that would help us?"

Gidget shrugged apologetically. "Unfortunately, we've checked his personal calendar. He never marks down when he visits his mistress. Pretty smart of him, in fact."

Jinlei rolled her eyes. Of all the things he could be smart about, that was the one thing he chose.

"Call me old-fashioned, but maybe there's a non-technological way we can know for sure when Su Hanjin will visit," Chains said languidly from his spot on the floor.

Despite Jinlei's feelings toward Chains at the moment, she was willing to hear him out if it will help them move things faster. "How?" she asked.

Chains gave a lopsided grin. "Go to the source. The mistress herself."

Jinlei and Gidget looked at each other. Why hadn't they thought of that before?

"I don't think she'll talk that easily," Kai said.

Chains shrugged. "We'll make her talk." Then he broke out in a devilish grin. "I have an even better idea."

Jinlei peered at him suspiciously. "What?"

"We make *you* Su Hanjin's mistress." Chains grinned, his teeth looking like fangs.

* * *

When Chains first suggested that Jinlei be Su Hanjin's mistress, she thought his brain had really fallen out of his head, and she had a mind to slap it back in. But after careful discussion, they realized that it was actually a good plan, ensuring that they would entrap Su Hanjin without giving him recourse to escape.

Gidget set to work, finding out as much as she could about the mistress. Soon, she had a full report.

"Alright," Gidget announced to the room. "Zhang Chun Hua, also known by her gamer name, Seraphine. Twenty-two years old. A struggling gamer and cosplayer." Gidget's screen showed the glamorous young lady they saw with Su Hanjin at the café. The photo showed her modelling a game character. The detail was impeccable, from the flamboyant hot pink hairstyle, to the form-fitting leather clothing, to the little accessories she wore. "She dropped out of college to pursue her passion for gaming and cosplaying. But it wasn't as easy as she thought, hence the need for a patron like Su Hanjin." Gidget clacked a few more keys and showed them the next set of data. "They met at a gaming competition, where Corp. X Entertainment was a sponsor. She was a competitor and also a model for the competition's promotions. She was eliminated in the first round but still left with a huge prize." Gidget winked at them. "There are monthly payments wired to her account, enough to pay her living expenses and extra toys she wants. The payments come from a subsidiary of Corp. X."

"Alright. So how are we going to persuade her to help us?" Jinlei asked.

"Bring her back here," Wang Bai instructed. "We know from the data that she frequently goes to the internet and gaming café close to her apartment. You can intercept her there."

"With pleasure." Chains grinned devilishly.

* * *

Jinlei, Chains, Gidget and Kai filed into Wang Bai's van. Wang Bai and Chem stayed behind to look after Jun. Kai drove.

Gidget waited in the van, surveilling them. Jinlei, Chains and

Kai were outfitted with mics. They knew Seraphine often came to the internet and gaming café in the late afternoon. The same café they always frequented.

The three of them only had to wait a few minutes in the café when Seraphine walked in the door. Chains waited until she settled into a gaming station, and he took up the station next to her. Jinlei and Kai watched them from the corner of their eyes. They heard Chains through their earpieces.

Chains was playing the same first-person shooter game as Seraphine. They heard her give a cry of frustration.

"Man, she really sucks," Gidget said in their ears. "Don't know what made her think she could do this for a living."

"How bad is she?" whispered Jinlei.

"Bad," Gidget said. "I'm playing the game right now too. She makes amateur mistakes."

They all quieted when Chains started talking. "Ooh, that must have hurt."

"Shut up," Seraphine told him off.

Chains made further attempts at conversation, all resulting in Seraphine ignoring him.

"Dude ain't doing too well," Kai remarked.

Jinlei glanced over at them. Seraphine was sitting on the edge of her seat to the right, leaning as far away as she could from Chains, who was sitting on her left. For all his big talk, it looked like Chains wasn't as skilled at talking to the ladies as Jinlei had thought. Perhaps they had sent in the wrong person.

"Listen," Chains tried talking to Seraphine again. "Why don't you join my team? We can kill those other guys and increase our experience points."

Jinlei saw Seraphine shift a little bit. From what Jinlei could gather, Chains wasn't a bad player at all—not as good as Gidget, but certainly better than Seraphine. Chains's suggestion seemed to pique Seraphine's interest. Probably out of desperation.

And then Chains had to ruin it.

"Do you play support? Coz you just gave my heart a power boost," Chains said. Jinlei could imagine him giving a goofy grin.

"Oh no, Chains . . ." Gidget said over the mic.

Seraphine retorted, "No thanks. Looks like you're beyond saving." And with that, she stood up to leave.

Jinlei and Kai shared a look, and they both ran out of the café ahead of Seraphine. They intercepted Seraphine outside.

"Seraphine?" Jinlei started.

Seraphine paused and looked around. There were a few people in the streets, but right beside them was a dead-end alleyway. The same alleyway where Kai had attacked her and Su Hanjin earlier. She recognized Kai's red hair and started to back away. But she couldn't go too far as she bumped into Chains while she was backtracking. She looked visibly nervous.

"Who are you people? What do you want?" Seraphine asked shakily.

"Please," Jinlei tried to reassure her. "We just want to talk. If you'll come quietly with us, this doesn't have to get complicated."

Seraphine made the unfortunate move to run away. Chains quickly grabbed her and put a cloth doused with chlorophyll over her mouth. Once she was out, they hurried back to the van.

XXIII

Seraphine awoke with a start. She was lying down on a ratty old sofa and bolted upright. Dazed and confused, she scanned the room and the faces around her. She trembled like a scared little rabbit.

They were back at Wang Bai's basement. Wang Bai had an old sofa stored somewhere in one of the rooms, and Chains and Kai carried it over to the computer room. It was getting a bit crowded there with not enough seating.

Jinlei approached Seraphine gently and handed her a glass of water as a sign of peace. Seraphine didn't take it.

Jinlei winced, feeling immense guilt at what they had to do. But they didn't have much of a choice—time was of the essence. And of all people, Seraphine would for sure be able to help them, even let them know any weaknesses Su Hanjin had that they could exploit to their advantage.

"Please," Seraphine spoke. "I'll give you what you want. Just let me go. You want money?"

Kai let out a sneering breath. "No. But what we want is where your money comes from."

Seraphine's lips trembled in confusion.

"Su Hanjin," Kai said to clarify.

Seraphine's eyes widened, and she started to inch back into the sofa.

Jinlei knelt down beside her and spoke softly, "He's hurt my friend—our friend. We need to get a particular medicine from him to cure our friend. All we want is to meet with him and for him to give us what we need. For our friend."

Seraphine somewhat eased but still looked around uncertainly. She settled on Jinlei, examining every inch of her face. She took a deep breath and finally said less shakily, "So you want me to arrange a meeting with him?"

Jinlei chewed her lip and looked to Wang Bai, who nodded in encouragement. "When will you meet him next?"

Seraphine shrugged. "He hasn't called me lately. Sometimes he does that. He's busy, you know."

"Could you arrange a meeting?"

Seraphine cocked her head uncertainly. "I think so."

Jinlei let out a breath. The glamorous gamer had agreed to the first part of the plan. Now for the trickier part. "Alright. Could you tell him to meet you at your apartment tonight?"

Seraphine nodded. "Yeah."

"And then, instead of you, it shall be me who shall be there," Jinlei said, holding her breath.

Seraphine stared at Jinlei for what felt like a long time. "You'll be waiting at my apartment for him?"

"And me," said Kai.

Seraphine sat up straight, her defenses up again.

Jinlei spoke quickly to appease her. "I know this may seem unusual, but . . ."

Seraphine interrupted, "If all you really want is the medicine, why do you need to meet him at my apartment?"

Jinlei's cheeks flushed, and she looked to the others for help.

"That's not really what you want, is it?" Seraphine asked, her voice rising a pitch. "You plan to do something with him!"

"No," Jinlei insisted. She tried to gently touch Seraphine's arm, but Seraphine jerked her arm away. "It's true that we want the medicine to cure our friend. It's just that I don't think he'll willingly give it to us."

Seraphine gave a mirthless laugh. "Of course not. Why would he want to deal with a bunch of lowlifes? You have no idea who you're dealing with."

Kai knelt down and placed his face intimidatingly close to Seraphine's. "I don't think *you* know who you're dealing with. Do you know what he did? He injected a drug that turned our—I mean, her friend into a demon. What kind of person does that?"

Seraphine was silent.

Kai stared at her. Hard. "I'll tell you. It's the kind of middle-aged sleazeball who would prey on young girls in need of money. I hope it was worth it."

Seraphine gasped and slapped Kai across the face.

Jinlei pulled Kai back and tried to reason with Seraphine once again. "As crudely as he put it, he's right. Su Hanjin is not a good person. My friend wasn't the only one. There were others." She gulped, remembering how close she was to being turned into a semi-devil herself if Chains hadn't rescued her. Chains . . . she'll deal with her confusing thoughts regarding him later. "I saw them with my own eyes. Su Hanjin and Corp. X—they're abducting people off the streets and experimenting on them. I don't know for what reason, but it can't be good. We have to stop him. Please. Will you help us?"

Seraphine looked away from Jinlei. She was still tight-lipped.

Wang Bai came over to them. "I think it's best we let her think about it for a while. Come, you must be hungry."

Wang Bai asked Chem to buy some food for all of them. He came back with take-out containers and enough food for everyone. They all ate in silence.

After they were done eating, Seraphine spoke up first. "Where is he now? Your friend?"

"Would you like to see him?" asked Jinlei.

Seraphine hesitated, then nodded.

They took her to the next room, where Jun was still asleep. Chem said he was recovering nicely. His pulse and his vitals were getting back to normal. He could wake up anytime soon.

Seraphine didn't seem too surprised when she saw Jun, but she staggered back, nevertheless.

"We can't let him keep doing this," Jinlei urged her.

Seraphine gulped. "It wasn't just for the money, you know," she said, as if seeking absolution.

Jinlei didn't much care what Seraphine did with her own life but let her talk. Seraphine looked like she just needed someone to listen to her.

Seraphine continued, "I had never had anyone pay attention to me that way. Most people just care about my looks. That's why I became a cosplayer, even though I had no interest in it. I don't really like being in the spotlight, you know. I wanted to be a gamer. But whenever I went to these conventions, people would always ask me to pose and take pictures with them and ask me why I was not in costume. One day one of the convention organizers offered to pay me to dress up and model a character for them. I agreed coz I needed the money. Soon, I got more popularity and money from cosplaying than doing the thing I actually wanted to do." She put her hands in her pockets sheepishly. "But when I met Su Hanjin . . . he seemed like he really cared. He asked me questions about myself. Asked me about my hopes and dreams. And supported me in what I wanted to do. He still supports me. No one else had ever done that for me. Not even my own parents."

Jinlei's heart ached for her. Jinlei knew what it was like to be all alone. And if she hadn't met the right people in time . . . she shuddered to think what would have become of her. Maybe she would have fallen into the same trap as Seraphine had. She touched Seraphine gently on the shoulder.

"I'm glad he was good to you. But I'm sure you know of Corp. X's reputation and, by extension, Su Hanjin's. Though he might have shown you a better side of himself, his hands are far from clean. But you have a chance to make things right." Jinlei set her jaw firmly and said emphatically, "If you're worried about what comes after, I can personally assure you, you'll have a soft place to land right here. If it weren't for them, I don't know where I'd be today." She swept her hand across all the faces who had helped her thus far. One look at Chains and Wang Bai, and she knew they had already reconciled and forgiven each other. Despite the harsh words exchanged earlier, they had proven to each other that they were true friends. The road to Dao Fai will be long and hard. And they will need to trust each other through it all.

Wang Bai concurred, "We've helped countless others like yourself. If you're willing, I'm sure we can find a place for someone with your charm and skills."

"I can even teach you a thing or two about gaming," Gidget

grinned and pointed to herself. "Gidget."

Seraphine's eyes widened with pleasant surprise. "*You're* the Gidget? I can't believe it. You're one of the top players in 'Full Metal Combat,' even beating some of the pros. Come to think of it, why haven't you gone pro?"

Gidget shrugged. "I'm not really in it for the money. Besides, I'm preoccupied with other more interesting things at the moment." She gave Seraphine a sly grin. "So what do you say? Will you help us? Even just this once."

Seraphine chewed her lip as she thought. "Okay," she finally said.

XXIV

Seraphine and Su Hanjin sent messages back and forth before she finally convinced him to meet her at her apartment that night. The rendezvous will happen at midnight.

Seraphine remotely added Jinlei and Kai's palm prints to her security scanner. Seraphine stayed behind in Wang Bai's basement with Chem, who would continue to look after Jun.

Wang Bai parked on the other side of the street of Seraphine's apartment. Jinlei, Kai and Chains moved in the shadows. Jinlei unlocked the main door of Seraphine's building with her palm print and let everyone in. The low-rise building was unpretentious and utilitarian. It was a building that did what it was supposed to do—provided shelter from the elements. Nothing more, nothing less. A far cry from the shiny gilded ornaments of the Corp. X building.

"Sheesh. You'd think with all his money, Su Hanjin would provide his girlfriend with better accommodations," Chains commented, clucking his tongue.

Jinlei was inclined to agree. "This just shows the type of character he is. His greediness knows no bounds."

Jinlei and Kai proceeded to the fifth floor, where Seraphine's apartment was. Chains stayed behind in the lobby, dressed like a night watch patrolling the building.

Jinlei placed her palm on the scanner attached to Seraphine's door, and the door magically unlocked.

Despite the stark and gray conditions of the building, Seraphine's apartment unit was anything but. It was filled with colorful neon lights, the latest gadgets, and bespoke computer and gaming systems. Not to mention clothes, jewelry, cosmetics, and all manner of skincare. Her furniture was sparse, and there wasn't much in the way of kitchen accessories. Other than gaming and beauty, it looked like she had little interest in anything else.

Jinlei settled herself in position. She sat on the edge of Seraphine's bed, the side furthest from the bedroom door. She had her back to the door and donned one of Seraphine's colorful wigs for cosplaying. That way, Su Hanjin wouldn't recognize her until he was close enough to her and she could immobilize him. Chains hid in the coat closet by the front door.

"Depraved billionaire at one o'clock," Gidget's voice came into Jinlei's ear.

"Copy," Jinlei murmured into her mic.

Seraphine's apartment building only had two entrance and exit points—the main entrance at the front of the building and the back entrance.

"His car's parked right outside the entrance," Gidget informed everyone. "There's one bodyguard watching the entrance from the car. The other is outside the back entrance. Two of them accompanied him upstairs."

"I'll be ready for them both in the lobby," Chains's voice floated through the receiver.

Jinlei took a deep breath. Her heart started to pound heavily, and she gave her jittery body a little shake. But she couldn't easily shake away the uneasy feeling piercing through her bones. She told herself it was normal to be nervous with Jun's welfare at stake.

Soft beeping sounds sounded from the door before it opened. Jinlei clamped her fists to stop them from shaking. *This is it*, she thought.

Slow, deliberate footsteps came behind her, then stopped just outside the bedroom door.

Jinlei whirled around to confront that monster of a man, expecting him to be surprised. But she received the surprise instead. She doubled back in uncertainty. First of all—he didn't seem at all surprised to see her.

There was something else different about Su Hanjin. He looked bigger, his muscles bulging underneath his fancy suit. His facial features were more pronounced, the bones jutting out of his skin. His teeth were sharper, his eyes more diluted. He looked more . . . devilish.

Jinlei was doused with a cold dose of terror. He couldn't have given himself the drug? No, that couldn't be. Su Hanjin seemed like the kind of person who would experiment on others but not on himself. She put on her fiercest look and demanded, "Give me the antidote for the Diablocyte-X, and I'll let you live."

Su Hanjin guffawed like an obnoxious hyena. "You've got guts, little girl. I'll tell you that." He looked her up and down. "It's a shame. A pretty one like you. If you weren't such a pain in my backside, I'd have you for myself."

Jinlei suppressed a shudder and instead channeled it into action. In the blink of an eye, she was right in front of Su Hanjin. Her legs encircled him with a roundhouse kick. But it didn't land as he blocked it and countered with a blow across her face.

Jinlei doubled back in shock. She hadn't expected him to possess any fighting skill.

At that moment, Kai burst out of the closet door, running to tackle the offensive man. When Jinlei saw them at the auction, Su Hanjin was cowering behind his bodyguard as Kai fought with impressive skill and strength. This time was different. Su Hanjin matched Kai's blows and parries, ending with a kick across Kai's face. Kai staggered backward, managing to stay on his feet.

The fighting came to a momentary truce, and Su Hanjin spoke, "I do like that look in your eyes, Xu Kai. Like a deer caught in headlights knowing the car's coming to crush him."

Kai rubbed the side of his cheek that was hit. "I must say, I didn't expect that of you. I didn't think you were man enough to try your own experiments on yourself. But why does it have a different effect on you than the others?"

Su Hanjin pumped out his chest with pride. "I only injected a small dose on myself and my bodyguards—just enough to give us demonic levels of strength and vitality, but not enough to completely turn us into semi-devils."

Kai scoffed contemptuously. "As I thought, you weren't really man enough to inject yourself with the full dosage."

"On the contrary," Su Hanjin countered, "There's 'man enough' as you say, and there's stupidity. I'm not stupid enough to inject myself completely with a still-experimental drug."

Before things could get out of hand again, Jinlei hastily interrupted and tried to appeal to Su Hanjin's reason, "Please. We'll go quietly if you just give us the antidote."

Su Hanjin suppressed a chuckle. "Oh, you are a precious one, aren't you? I do have the antidote, but I won't give it to you. What I could do instead is deliver your friend's brains and guts to you. How's that?"

Jinlei scowled in confusion.

"Ah!" Su Hanjin snapped his fingers. "Didn't you know? Every Corp. X experiment has a chip implanted into their bodies. These experiments could go horribly wrong after all. The subjects could prove destructive to society. We, as scientists, must always have full control of our subjects. Therefore, we've developed a truly innovative nano-device, a miniaturized plasma generator, should our subjects prove uncontrollable. A kill switch, in short."

Jinlei trembled with the cold rush running throughout her body. What kind of monster truly was he? Her mouth was left dry, speechless in shock.

Su Hanjin gazed upon her with his lecherous eyes. "Sadly, we didn't have time to put one on you. But we managed to put one on him," he pointed to Kai, "and your other friend."

Su Hanjin turned to Kai, breaking out in a wide, sleazy smile. "And this is the thanks I get after showing you mercy. The only reason you're alive right now, dear boy, is because I've allowed it. I could have exploded your insides out at any given moment. Instead, I've let you live."

Kai didn't say anything and was frozen in place. Only his fists quivered—out of anger or fear, Jinlei wasn't sure.

"Since I am a businessman, I'll make you a deal," Su Hanjin said in his oily voice, dripping with scornful jeering. "You come back with me to Corp. X to continue our experiments with you both and I won't kill your friend. How about it? We all get what we want."

Jinlei saw red, almost blinded with flashing hatred toward the odious man. Before she could retort anything back, Kai rushed at him with a series of blows in rapid succession. It didn't take long for Jinlei to join in.

Jinlei and Kai fought with all the strength and skill of their vast experience and training, yet they still felt wildly outclassed. A far cry from the Su Hanjin of earlier.

The fighting extended beyond Seraphine's bedroom and into the living area with all the expensive technology and gadgets. Jinlei was thrown against Seraphine's gaming set-up, the monitors crashing against her weight. A sharp pain jabbed along her back as she lay on top of the toppled desk and broken monitors. She groaned.

Jinlei briefly saw stars. Amidst the blur, she saw Su Hanjin smash Chains's head against Seraphine's vanity mirror, the lightbulbs around it fizzing out.

The loud crashes and bangs around the apartment must have alerted the bodyguards outside, and they barged in, helping their master.

Against a trio of drug-enhanced opponents, it wasn't long before Jinlei and Chains were overpowered into submission.

Jinlei gritted her teeth. Seeing no other way out in the meantime, she opted to bargain with the devil himself. "If we go with you, promise me you'll give the antidote to Jun."

"No, don't do it," Gidget's voice crackled into Jinlei's ear.

Su Hanjin cocked his head, pretending to think. "You strike a hard bargain, little girl, but deal. I'll give your friend the antidote if you'll give me back my Seraphine."

Seraphine. It was then that something in Jinlei's mind clicked. "Did she tell you we were coming?"

Su Hanjin's sleazy lips curled into a sneer, and he grabbed Jinlei's hair, forcing her to look at him. She didn't wince and looked at him with all the contempt she could muster. "Of course, she did. You underestimate her. And me. You think you can play your little games with us?" He violently let go of her hair and nodded at his bodyguards.

"Take them."

"Wait!" Jinlei called out before it was too late. "Where's the antidote?"

Su Hanjin regarded her carefully, then smiled. "You really are a spitfire, aren't you? Have your people meet my people in front of the Corp. X building in an hour. Bring Seraphine."

Wang Bai's voice sounded in Jinlei's ear. "We'll be there in an hour and find a way to break you out. Hang in there, you two. Chains, retreat back to the van."

"Lobby is still clear. Be there in a minute," Chains answered.

XXV

Su Hanjin's bodyguards placed electronic handcuffs on Jinlei and Kai's wrists. One of the bodyguards made a call to headquarters to send for a van. The van arrived within minutes, and they were all escorted downstairs. Su Hanjin drove back to Corp. X headquarters in his own luxury car with his two bodyguards, while the other two bodyguards threw Jinlei and Chains in the back of the van like the kidnapping victims they were.

Jinlei shook in disbelief. Seraphine had betrayed them. Her thoughts raced through her mind, she barely heard what was going on in her earpiece. She started paying attention when Wang Bai, Gidget and Chains sounded like they were back in the basement confronting Seraphine.

"How could you?" Gidget spoke first.

"Now we're even," Seraphine's voice, more muffled, sputtered in Jinlei's ear.

"What do you mean, even?" asked Gidget.

"I did . . . *crackle* . . . arrange the meeting like you asked me to. But the rest . . . well, that's for taking me hostage."

Chains said in a low, dangerous voice. "Bad news, missy. News flash: you're at our mercy now. We could do with you what we want, and no one will hear you scream."

Jinlei knew Chains was merely scaring Seraphine and wouldn't do anything to her because they needed her to trade for the antidote. None of them knew how much Su Hanjin had told Seraphine about what he was planning and the trade they'd negotiated. Their mics and nano-cameras only fed to Wang Bai's unmarked van and not to the basement computers.

Jinlei's receiver fizzled and she wasn't sure if that was a laugh that came from Seraphine or distorted static.

Seraphine said, "No, you won't. You're going to take me to Corp. X if you want your two friends to live."

Chains bluffed, "We've broken into the Corp. X building before, and we can do it again. We don't really need you. In fact, no one does. You could disappear, and no one would miss you."

Seraphine seemed unfazed as she responded coolly, "Wrong again, you pathetic bleached blonde gone wrong, looking like it was dyed by a preschool art class. You will take me to Corp. X because I can tell you just how to take down Su Hanjin himself. That's what you losers want, isn't it?"

Chains snorted. "You just betrayed us to him. What makes you think we'll believe you now?"

Seraphine shrugged. "Fine. Like you said, no one will probably miss me when I'm gone. You have a lot more to lose than I do. It's up to you—take the risk with me or kill me now, and you'll never know how to take down Su Hanjin himself."

There was a palpable silence in Jinlei's receiver. She glanced at Kai nervously. He scowled back.

Wang Bai finally spoke, "Chains will take you to Corp. X. Wire up."

* * *

Jinlei and Kai arrived at Corp. X, the guards handling them roughly as they were escorted to the research lab. In a sordid twist of irony, they were exactly back from where they so desperately tried to escape.

The men and women in the white coats surrounded them, waiting for them. It looked as if the researchers were alerted of their arrival beforehand.

Su Hanjin was in the center of the white coats. "Strap them in," he commanded.

The bodyguards helped the researchers roughly put Jinlei and Kai onto the beds. No matter how much they resisted, the bodyguards were stronger. Two bodyguards pinned down each of them as the metal straps attached to the bed securely strapped them in.

The white coats gathered around them and conferred with each other. Others were on the computers. Others were preparing the Diablocyte-X, drawing it from a vial with a syringe.

Jinlei struggled against the cool hard metal restraints around her, but it was no use. There was no wiggle room between her and the restraints.

Her captors failed to check them for any surveillance equipment, and her and Kai's nano-surveillance technology was too small for anyone to detect. Jinlei still heard the buzz of conversation between Seraphine and the others in her ear. It sounded like they were close to Corp. X. A car door slammed, footsteps crunched on the gravel pavement, then voices.

"Do you have the antidote?" It was Chains's voice.

An unfamiliar voice responded, "Give us the girl first."

Seraphine spoke up, "Take us inside. To Su Hanjin's office."

A mocking laughter sounded. "Fat chance, little girl. Don't think you have any power here just because you're Mister Su Hanjin's plaything. Our instructions were clear: we take you—and only you, and we can give this pathetic excuse for a vagrant the antidote."

"Why don't you call Su Hanjin's office and check?" Seraphine replied.

There were some grunts and protests, but it seemed to Jinlei that they were escorted into the building to Su Hanjin's office.

Jinlei had to give up listening in on Chains and Seraphine as the white coats with the syringes dangerously approached them.

Su Hanjin grinned his toothy, diabolical grin. "These are the perfect experimental subjects. We need soldiers like them with spunk and superior fighting skills. If the drug works on them, they'll surely be part of our elite forces. Give it to 'em!"

Kai thrashed about in his restraints, though it was not much use. Instead, he growled and yelled at them to get their attention. "Hey! You want to see what a real elite soldier looks like? Why don't you try it on me first? The girl is all talk, but when it comes down to it, she ain't much."

"Hey!" Jinlei protested. Even though she knew Kai said that to buy them some time, she still resented the insinuation.

"Why do you think I always have to be around, huh?" Kai continued. "She won't be able to defeat anyone on her own."

The hairs on Jinlei's back prickled up. She could tolerate some insults done out of good intentions, but Kai was starting to cross the line!

Su Hanjin chuckled affectionately. "Why, isn't that sweet? I thought you two were just working together. I didn't know you were so close. Ah . . . young love. There really is nothing like the vibrance of youth. Young girls are really the best, aren't they."

Su Hanjin directed his lecherous gaze at Jinlei, his eyes shining with depravity.

Jinlei would have screamed at him if Kai hadn't spoken first.

"You're right," Kai said, his eyes equally shining wickedly. "I'll make you a deal. If you inject me with the stuff first, you can have her all to yourself."

"What?" Jinlei gasped, barely able to comprehend what Kai had just said.

Su Hanjin lifted an eyebrow. "What might you mean, oh sneaky one?"

Kai grinned. "To tell you the truth, I was disappointed the first time when the drug didn't work. Who wouldn't want to be all powerful? I can see why you tried the stuff on yourself. Besides, if you're stupid enough to give me, the person who's trying to kill you, a drug that will increase my powers, you can't blame anyone but yourself when I finally kill you using your own experiment. And that's just sweet, poetic justice."

Su Hanjin's condescending grin twitched. Kai's words must have really struck a nerve as Su Hanjin immediately commanded the white coats to administer the drug to Kai.

One of the white coats with the syringe inserted the needle into Kai's arm. They waited for a few minutes. As before, nothing happened.

"Well? Why's nothing happening?" Su Hanjin barked.

The white coats cowered in obsequiousness as they rushed to confer among themselves.

"Sir." Jinlei recognized the same woman with the tablet from before. "It's just like before. The drug doesn't seem to work on him."

"And why not?" Su Hanjin demanded.

The white coats all erupted with their own theories as to why the drug wouldn't work on Kai to try to appease Su Hanjin.

"Perhaps there's something in his biology."

"Perhaps he carries a rare gene that renders him immune to the drug."

"Perhaps he has certain antibodies that fight the drug."

"Well, what are you waiting for?" Su Hanjin angrily bellowed. "Check him right away!"

The white coats scrambled to gather samples of Kai's DNA, swabbing the inside of his mouth, scraping his skin and plucking his hair.

"Ow! Hey! You don't need more than one strand of hair!" Kai shouted at them.

The scientists were hard at work analyzing samples of Kai's DNA.

"Well?" Su Hanjin impatiently asked.

The woman with the tablet answered, "We have the most advanced genetic testing technology in the world. It shouldn't take more than a few minutes."

Just then, all the lights turned off, as well as all the computers and everything else in the room. There was a power outage.

With the loss of power, the restraints holding Jinlei unbuckled itself, and Jinlei jumped out of the bed without hesitation. Just in time, too, as the power was only out for a minute before coming back on again. But by then, it was too late. For Su Hanjin and the scientists, that is.

Kai and Jinlei wasted no time grabbing hold of the scientists and throwing them across the room. Kai went after Su Hanjin. They threw and exchanged blows as the expensive equipment around them crashed and shattered.

Chains came bounding into the room, ready to rescue them, when he realized they didn't need all that much rescuing.

"Chains!" Jinlei called out to him when she saw him.

"We gotta get out of here right away," Chains told Jinlei in the rush.

"I agree. Do you have the antidote?"

Chains shook his head. "Not yet . . ."

Before Chains could finish, all came to a stop when a new set of men in suits came in.

"Su Hanjin!" one of them called out, the most self-important and pompous-looking one.

Su Hanjin and Kai paused their fighting and slowly turned toward the voice. At the sight of the tall and severe-looking man, Su Hanjin looked positively incensed.

"Xia Jielun. What brings you here?" Su Hanjin asked.

The tall and severe-looking man with the slick-backed hair bared his teeth in a sneer that looked strangely triumphant. "Someone called me here, saying it was important—that I had to take care of things as everything was going to the toilet. I heard *you* had mismanaged Project D-X, and now, I have to fix it."

Su Hanjin remained composed. "I assure you, everything is under control."

Xia Jielun laughed. "Yes, I can see that," he said, his voice dripping with sarcasm.

Su Hanjin waved his hand offhandedly as if the chaotic mess would disappear with a gesture of his hand. "This is just a minor hiccup."

"That's not what I heard," Xia Jielun said. "I heard this project is draining money. You've been over-budgeting and inflating financial reports to deviate funds from the company to your pathetic little pet project. Not to mention the shell companies you've set up to cover up the complex layers of financial transactions for all the money you've embezzled over the years."

Su Hanjin's face turned a bright shade of red. "How dare you accuse me?" he barked.

Xia Jielun scoffed. "Oh, I'm not accusing you. I know this for a fact."

Su Hanjin narrowed his eyes. "How can you be so sure?"

Xia Jielun broke out in a triumphant grin. "Your wife told me.

In fact, she's right here, in your office. Shall we take care of this in a more private manner? No need to involve the employees."

Without another word, Su Hanjin stalked off, shouldering Xia Jielun as he passed by the tall executive.

Xia Jielun regarded the trembling employees. "As you were. As usual, no word of this gets out, or we'll bury you in legal proceedings. Don't forget, you've all signed a non-disclosure agreement." He turned toward the other men in suits he came in with. "Help them clean up this mess."

Xia Jielun nodded at Chains as if they knew each other. Chains gestured to Jinlei and Kai for them to follow Xia Jielun and Su Hanjin. Jinlei looked at Chains questioningly.

"It was all Seraphine," Chains whispered to Kai and Jinlei as they made their way to Su Hanjin's office. "She called Su Hanjin's wife and introduced herself as his mistress. In a fit of anger, his wife called her young nephew, that guy Xia Jielun, and told him all about what her husband was up to. I don't really know all the details, but long story short, Su Hanjin's position in the family has always been shaky because he's only related to them by marriage and not by blood. There are always others waiting in the wings to take him down. The only reason he rose up this high was because he was actually really smart and capable, and his wife was one of the patriarch's favorite grandchildren. But now that he's betrayed his wife, his wife is apparently feeding him to the wolves." Chains whistled, his finger making little circles, indicating he thought the Xia family was out of their minds.

Kai chuckled in delight.

Jinlei shook her head at the messiness of the Xia family. They weren't very pleasant to begin with, but she never expected their clan to devolve this much into depravity.

When they reached Su Hanjin's office, his angry wife started throwing things at him—vases, porcelain displays, expensive artwork, a computer, anything she could get her hands on.

At first, Su Hanjin graciously took his wife's abuse as he dodged the oncoming flying objects. But his patience could only last for so long as he eventually grabbed hold of his wife's wrists to restrain her. She spat at him in spite. He flung her wrists away and angrily wiped the spit off his face.

"Get a hold of yourself, woman!" Su Hanjin commanded.

"Go to hell!" she screamed at him.

Su Hanjin's grotesque facial muscles throbbed in fury, and he raised his hand as if to strike his wife.

"Watch yourself, you disgusting social climber," Xia Jielun warned. "Do not lay a hand on my aunt if you know what's good for you."

Su Hanjin clenched his wide jaw and reluctantly brought down his hand.

Xia Jielun curled his lips in a disparaging smile. "My aunt was always too good for your sorry, peasant ass. We all warned her not to marry you. I don't know what you must have fed her to trick her into loving you. But you messed with the wrong family. You cross one of us, you cross all of us. This is the end for you, Su Hanjin."

Su Hanjin's wife emitted a high-pitched cackle. "I have all the evidence of your wrongdoings, you stupid fool! Not only will you be stripped of your title, status and position, we'll make sure you go away for a *very* long time, imprisoned in the worst institution in the country. You'll be left with nothing! Nothing!"

Xia Jielun added, "The best part is, I'll take over your position and reap the benefits of your hard work. Come to think of it, I really must thank you."

Unable to take it anymore, Su Hanjin howled in fury and lunged at his wife. But Kai intercepted him just in time, and they were back to trading blows in a zealous, one-on-one fight.

Xia Jielun protectively grabbed hold of his aunt, leading her out of the office. He nodded toward Chains and Seraphine. "I leave this to you to clean up this mess."

Seraphine saluted him good-naturedly. "You got it."

Su Hanjin's wife gave Seraphine a lingering, enigmatic look as if she didn't know if she should thank the mistress for revealing herself or hate her for doing so.

Jinlei and Chains went around Su Hanjin's office, opening and closing the drawers, looking for the antidote, while Kai kept Su Hanjin occupied.

"I don't know if he's actually keeping it in here," Jinlei said frantically.

"Over there," Chains pointed to Su Hanjin's secret room with the safe, the same room with the secret elevator they escaped with the last time they were here. "It's worth checking out."

Just as they were entering Su Hanjin's secret room, Seraphine was getting in the elevator with a bag stuffed with bills. Jinlei spotted the open safe, cleaned out of its contents. Her eyes widened in shock.

Seraphine stared back unapologetically. "See ya," was all she said before the elevator doors closed, making her clean escape.

Jinlei turned to Chains, pointing speechlessly at the elevator.

Chains sighed. "Let her be. It's not like Su Hanjin or Corp. X will miss the cash. She probably needs it more than they do. Let's just look for the antidote, okay?"

Jinlei wordlessly set to work, looking for the antidote. It definitely wasn't in the safe—Seraphine had emptied it out.

"AAAAGGGHHH!"

The commotion outside the secret room made Jinlei and Chains run back out to check on Su Hanjin and Kai.

Su Hanjin was on the ground, shaking and flailing. He looked smaller, crumpled on the ground. As Jinlei and Chains approached, they noticed his muscles were gone, as well as the sharp edges of his face. He was back to normal—back to the un-enhanced plain old executive that was Su Hanjin, who relied on his bodyguards to fight his fights. Except now, his bodyguards were nowhere to be found.

"I guess the drug has worn off. Lucky me." Kai cracked his knuckles, preparing for the final blow. Jinlei extended an arm to stop him.

"We still need the antidote," she reminded Kai. "You've stalled long enough. Give it to me now," she said to Su Hanjin, her voice devoid of any human warmth.

Su Hanjin looked up at them. From her vantage point, Jinlei thought he looked pitiful, like an abandoned small child.

"I'll give it to you, I promise," Su Hanjin said ingratiatingly. "But please—let me go. I promise I'll go away—far away! You'll never see or hear from me again. I have nothing left anyway . . ."

Jinlei ground her teeth, hardly believing his gall. He was still trying to weasel his way out of the consequences he must face after all the destruction he had caused. "I don't think you're in any position to negotiate," she said, her voice dripping with ice.

Su Hanjin's eyes glinted as if he still had something up his sleeve. "Fine. Just kill me now. And you'll never get the antidote."

Jinlei knelt down to face him. "Let me put it this way—either you give me the antidote now, and I'll give you a five-minute head start. You'll still have a chance of escaping—or—I'll give you over to Kai right now, and you don't even get a chance. So—what shall it be?"

A flash of anger fell across Su Hanjin's face. With trembling hands, he reached into his pocket and took out a tiny vial.

Jinlei grabbed it and clutched it tightly. "You have five minutes. Starting . . . now."

Without wasting another second, Su Hanjin bolted to the secret room and rushed into the elevator.

Kai grumbled at Jinlei for making him wait. But he showed his honor as a fighter and martial artist as he fulfilled his end of the bargain. He tapped his foot impatiently, looking at his watch. As soon as the five minutes were up, he dashed to the same elevator.

Over her earpiece, Jinlei heard Kai ask Gidget if she had eyes on Su Hanjin. Gidget tapped into the cameras surrounding the Corp. X building and relayed to Kai where Su Hanjin was running off to. It didn't take long before Kai caught up to Su Hanjin.

A blood-curdling scream pierced through Jinlei's earpiece. She shuddered and hastily took her earpieces out, unable to listen to Su Hanjin's wet, bloody screams.

Chains sighed. "Gotta hand it to the guy . . . he really did do what he said he'd do."

Jinlei turned away from Chains, not wanting him to see her tremble with immense guilt. She had seen her fair share of violence and killings. But everything she'd ever killed or witnessed being killed were demons and monsters—evil supernatural entities that took pleasure in harming and torturing human beings. In all her life, she never thought she could ever willingly lead a human being to their own slaughter. But in light of all Su Hanjin had done, not just to them, but to countless innocent victims—the kidnappings, the experiments, the druggings—she had caved to her baser nature. She could never forgive him for what he did to Jun.

She felt a gentle hand on her shoulder. "Don't think about it too much. Kai would have gotten to him sooner or later. You gave Su Hanjin the best chance he could—those five minutes were an act of mercy."

Jinlei tried to force a smile. "What I did—it went against every code of honor I was brought up to follow—the code of *xia*—the martial code of honor, as well as the shamanic code of honor. I'm supposed to protect human beings, not harm them."

"If it'll make you feel better, Su Hanjin was kind of a demon for a little while. And what he's done was really something a demon would do, not a human."

"You may be right," Jinlei reluctantly said, slumping her shoulders, unconvinced.

"We should head back. We still need to give Jun the antidote, don't we?"

"You're right," Jinlei agreed.

They boarded the elevator in Su Hanjin's secret room, then rode the van with Wang Bai and Gidget back to the herbal shop in silence.

XXVI

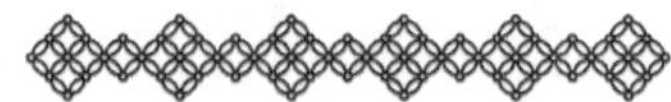

Back at Wang Bai's basement, they were all gathered around Jun, who had already woken up. Chem managed to keep him down by injecting him with large doses of tranquilizers. As soon as he got the antidote from Jinlei, Chem administered the cure to Jun.

"The effects shouldn't take long," Chem said. "He'll completely be back to normal by tomorrow."

"There's one other thing," Jinlei said. "Su Hanjin said they placed a chip in his body—a 'kill switch,' he said. Can we take it out?"

"Ah." Chem nodded. "Yes, they do that. If I remember correctly, the chip is embedded in the upper arm, near major blood vessels. It's very delicate with built-in anti-tampering features. Cutting anywhere near it could trigger it to activate. The extraction must be done with great care. Don't worry. We will take it out eventually."

"And how long will that take?" Jinlei asked, not bothering to cover up the edge in her voice.

"Soon," was all Chem said.

Jinlei crinkled her eyebrows in worry as she gazed upon Jun's sleeping face. The hard semi-devil features that marred his delicate beauty were starting to subside and traces of his normal face were starting to come back. At least they had managed to give him the antidote in time. She breathed deeply, letting the air slowly fill her lungs, forcing her body to slow down. Not only in the fighting arts, she was also trained in tai chi and meditative and mindfulness habits that really helped her ground herself and stay calm under immense pressure. With the air clearing away the dirty fog of her mind, she told herself that tomorrow would be a new day with new hope.

****

The next day, Jinlei rose bright and early, hardly able to contain herself. She had to see if Jun was okay. Gidget and Chains grumbled as they slowly woke up and got ready for the day while Jinlei urged them to hurry.

When they arrived at Wang Bai's basement, Jun was awake, sitting up on his bed. He looked a little worn down with slight dark circles under his eyes and looking visibly thinner and paler. Other than that, he looked to be completely back to normal.

Jinlei let out a relieved breath. Despite all her anxiousness over wanting to see him, she gingerly approached as if afraid that what she saw in front of her was merely an illusion, and she dared not hope too much.

Jun brightened when he saw her. "Lei-lei!"

Tears filled the brims of Jinlei's eyes. She fought the urge to run toward him and squeeze him tightly. Instead, she meekly peeped, "Jun?"

Either he was equally restraining himself out of propriety, or he was still too weak to move around too much, but Jun didn't move from his bed. "I'm so glad I finally found you," he said weakly.

Jinlei rushed to his side and sat on the edge of the bed. The others—Gidget, Chains, Wang Bai and Chem—crowded around him. "I'm so glad you're alright."

Jun looked around him, bewildered at all the unfamiliar faces. He rubbed his temples to soothe himself. "Who . . . and what . . . ? I woke up and found myself here and him," he nodded at Chem, "looking after me."

Jinlei smiled gently at him and told him all that happened since she arrived in the future. She spoke quickly, all the events rushing in her head. All the while, Jun kept silent, his eyes growing bigger and bigger at every revelation.

When she finally finished, he shook his head speechlessly. When he finally found the words, he said, "The last thing I remember was fighting with some men dressed in black suits. That must be— what did you say they were? Corp. X guards? After that, it was hazy. I do remember seeing you and the others and then being filled with uncontrollable rage, but it was disjointed, like a nightmare."

Jinlei bit her lip, the corners of her heart tugging, imagining what Jun must have gone through. He was always so full of color, vibrant with boundless energy. Now, he was blank and pale like a ghost just come back to life. He shouldn't have gone through all of that.

"But why are you here?" Jinlei asked, the inevitable question finally tumbling out of her.

"Your mother sent me," Jun said with a soft smile. "While the portal was still open, she asked me to look after you. I jumped in not long after you did. You didn't think she would send you all this way to fend solely for yourself, did you? But it looks like you found some help after all."

"Yes," Jinlei said, forcing herself not to think of her mother and her family back home because once she started, she didn't think she would be able to stop spiraling. "I was very fortunate to find friends and find my relatives. But now that you're here—did my mother tell you how to get back home?"

Jun sadly shook his head, and Jinlei's face fell.

"But she did give me a clue," Jun said.

Jinlei's breath caught in her throat. She noticed the others also lean in closer. "What is it?"

"Find the one who gives form to emptiness. And a word of caution—the time travel magic can only be used once. So make sure you do it right the first time."

Jinlei frowned thoughtfully.

Unable to take the silence anymore, Chains spoke up, "Great, another riddle. Emptiness to form? What does that mean? You'd think your own mother would help you out more."

"She did help me," Jinlei said resignedly, not having much energy to argue with Chains's outbursts. "All this time, she's been sending help my way—from Auntie Ying's messages passed down through generations to sending me Jun himself. Old Wang's earlier clue to 'find Li' must have meant 'find Jun' because she sent him to the future as well."

"Do you have any idea what this clue means?" Wang Bai asked.

Jinlei chewed thoughtfully on her lip. "Maybe . . ." she trailed off.

"Doesn't really matter," Gidget chirped cheerfully. "Either way, we'll help you. Are you ready for another adventure?"

It seemed an absurd question to ask anyone who had just gone through the fire and barely came out alive. But looking at all the eager faces around her, Jinlei knew she was in the right company of people who didn't scare easily and who loved living life on the edge as much as she did.

"I am if you are." Jinlei smiled.

Thank you for reading! Show your appreciation to the author by leaving a review on Amazon or Goodreads!

About the Author

PHOEBE AN LEE is a fantasy writer with a special interest in Asian mythology. She grew up watching anime and wuxia / xianxia, which greatly inspire her writing. She lives in daydream-land most of the time but is otherwise based in Toronto, Canada.

If you liked this book, also check out this
book by the author.

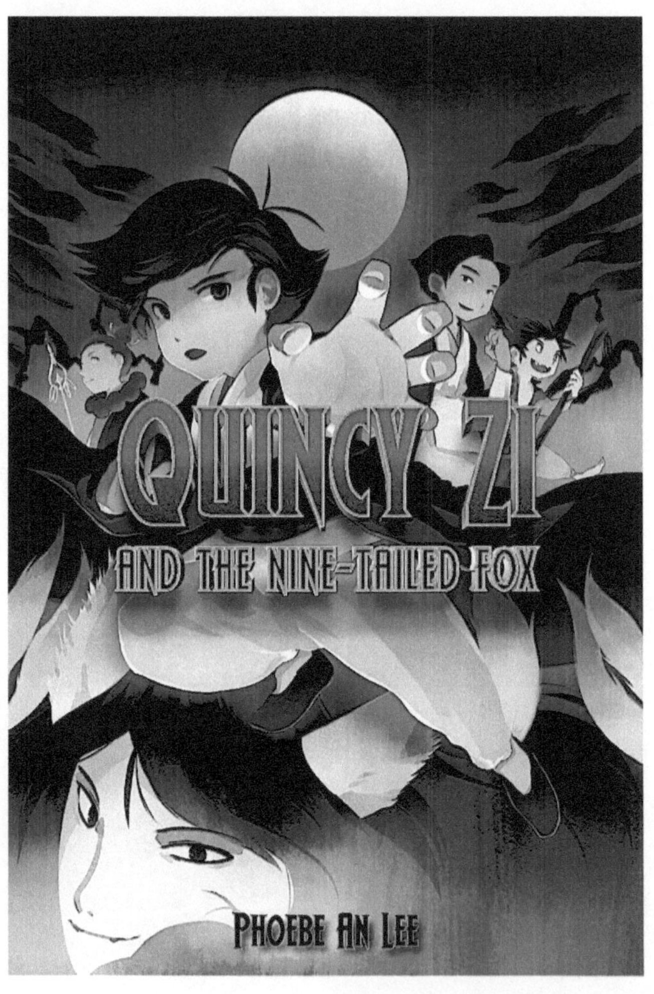